Ursula Pflug

DOWN FROM

Ursula Pflug's fiction and essays have appeared in numerous places in Canada, the US and the UK, including *Lightspeed, Fantasy, Strange Horizons, Postscripts, Leviathan, LCRW, Now Magazine,* and *The New York Review of Science Fiction.* She has collaborated extensively with filmmakers, playwrights, dancers and installation artists. Her work has been funded by The Ontario Arts Council, the Canada Council for the Arts and The Laidlaw Foundation. Her web presence can be found at http://ursulapflug.ca and at @ursulapflug.

Also by Ursula Pflug:

<u>Novels</u>
Motion Sickness
The Alphabet Stones
Green Music

<u>Short Fiction Collections</u>
Harvesting the Moon
After the Fires

SNUGGLY BOOKS

URSULA PFLUG

DOWN FROM

THIS IS A SNUGGLY BOOK

Copyright © 2018 by Ursula Pflug.
All rights reserved.

ISBN: 978-1-943813-57-5

Thanks to Tapanga Koe for reading and commenting on the ms., The Ontario Arts Council, The Canada Council for the Arts and Doug Back for material support over time, and Esther Pflug for insightful comments on the cover design.

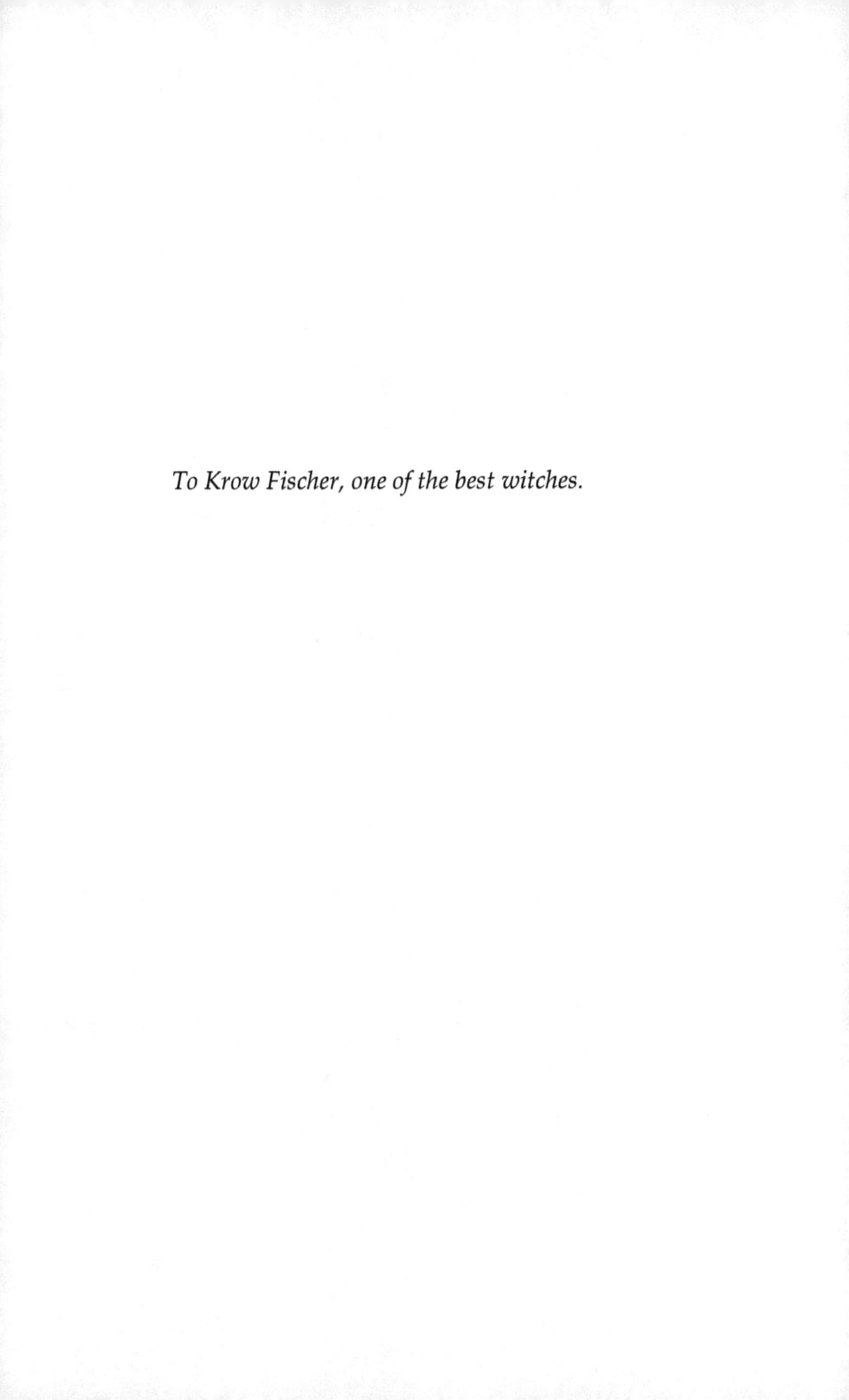

To Krow Fischer, one of the best witches.

DOWN FROM

CHAPTER ONE

It was dusk when Sandrine came down from the mountain and found Habib on the bridge in Brookside. She stood watching him fish; Habib, drenched in good looks, had always been watchable.

"Long drive?" she asked, when she was sure he knew she was there.

Fishing at Lock Eighteen was a practice favored mainly by folks who came up from the city. It was indeed a long drive, but people needed to get away from the heat and the sprawl, and if you weren't white you probably hadn't inherited a musty pasteboard cottage on one of the area's many lakes.

"Hi, Sandrine," he finally said. "Haven't seen you for a long time."

"Except in my dreams, Habib. We had sex not too long ago, in my dreams."

Habib smirked. "It being you, Sandrine, that probably counts."

"You mean you had that dream too?" It was a serious question, but Habib didn't answer. He looked at her cautiously, as if he was thinking.

The country was hot too, Sandrine figured, but it was a different kind of heat. It smelled good while it sweltered, unless you made the mistake of driving past a field where bio-solids had been pressed into service as fertilizer for the season's genetically engineered soy crop, thence to be turned into cattle feed, or perhaps soy burgers to be eaten by deluded teenage girls, who, while they were well versed in veganism, didn't know that GE foods including pre-made, heavily packaged soy burgers didn't require labeling in North America.

Sandrine shook her thick mop of blonde hair. She hadn't been back from the mountain for five minutes and already she was ranting, if only in her head. Still, it was good to know which world she'd landed in; clearly this was one where the shelves at the local supermarket were stocked with genetically modified organisms but you could still eat the fish you caught in the Brookside canal.

"What have you been doing lately?" Habib asked eventually.

"I've been up the mountain."

Habib looked puzzled for there were no mountains till you got to Appalachia, hundreds of miles to the south, or the Laurentians, far to the east, and you couldn't really call those mountains, they were more like big hills. He got an abstracted look and nodded, as if he'd just remembered she meant a different kind of mountain than those, a mountain that while real in its own way usually remained incorporeal.

"Want to go for coffee at the marina?" he finally asked.

She nodded. "We could."

"You sound hesitant."

She nodded again. "The problem really is that there is nothing left to say."

"You must have learned something."

"I guess."

"What did you learn?" he asked, more forcefully.

"I forget," Sandrine said truthfully.

Habib must have changed, she thought. Before, he would never have asked that; he'd just have flirted aimlessly. His hair was graying quite a bit but he was still handsome although not as slender as when they'd first met at one of her brother's parties in the city years before. Sandrine remembered how her eye used to follow him whether they were in the same room or on the same bridge. Catching herself, she'd be more careful, not wanting Habib to think she wanted to sleep with him. It wasn't that she'd never had sexual fantasies about Habib, because she had. Once, in fact, she'd had a dream in which, while they were making love, he'd transmogrified into a cyclopean arachnid.

She remembered sharing this story with her husband. She thought maybe his name was Randy.

"What's a cyclopean arachnid?" Might-Be-Randy had asked.

"I think it's something Atlantean but you should probably look it up," Sandrine had said.

She only realized later that her hubby had known neither what cyclopean nor arachnid meant. He hadn't been questioning the provenance of such a creature, for even formulating it in his mind as a creature at all had been quite beyond Randy's skills. Literacy, Sandrine had often noted, wasn't what it used to be. Shaking this new thought away, she reminded herself that both the dream and her conversation with her husband about it were just in her head. Possibly they weren't even real memories flicking through her mind as she looked at Habib, stood on his bridge, the water rushing beneath metal gates underneath.

A destabilizing thought, that one, but she had the feeling she'd had it before at another time very much like this one.

Habib's eyes were deep brown and a little lost and searching. Maybe he too felt they had once shared something important but couldn't quite remember what it was. Not sex, but some other form of intimacy. His weight gain and graying hair humanized him, Sandrine thought; he was no longer the angel, no longer glittered faintly like someone, like someone who—

"—has been up the mountain," he said.

"Did you just read my mind?" she asked.

He shrugged, as if it wasn't a big deal, but something they had often done together, much like having coffee at the marina. "Anyway, it's you who goes up, Sandrine, not me. You go on astral adventures, you come back."

"You're waiting for me when I come back," Sandrine said. Saying it, she knew it was true. "It's not precisely true that I go on adventures," she clarified. "In actuality I go up the mountain always, nowhere else."

"I saw you reappear at the first bend," he said.

She remembered then that no one else knew the path which to her was clear as day. The rest of them couldn't seem to see it, except Habib, and he only saw it a little.

"You could go too," she said, as she had before.

"Let's go for coffee instead," Habib said as it was possible he always did.

"To the marina?" she asked.

He shrugged, a little irritably. "Why not right there? It's better for watching the sun go down." He pointed to the little gift and bait shop overlooking the bridge and the lock. There were rooms for rent upstairs, mainly used by people like Habib who came from the city to fish on the canal. Sandrine had never been in the rooms although she had fantasies about them. She already lived on water; her house backed onto a mucky creek, but during spring mosquito season she often wanted to get away from the swamp, and then she'd play little movies through her head.

What if I had that life instead of this one? A little apartment, overlooking the canal? On break I could come downstairs and sit on the wooden porch at one of the little tables, stubbing out my cheap First Nations cigarettes in a big ceramic ashtray, something chic and retro from the fifties or sixties with a splatter glaze in turquoise, say, or orange, or best yet, both.

Sandrine didn't smoke anymore, but it seemed like an appropriate part of this fantasy. "If you can see the path, you can walk it," she said.

Habib leant his tackle against the bridge. "From the porch I can see it," he explained.

"The path?"

He knew she wasn't making fun of him, not really. She needed him too much to do that. "I meant my stuff."

"Ah, of course," she said. "Unlike at the marina."

"The cloud forests," he asked as they walked the few steps from the bridge to the store, "what are they like?"

"Made of thought like everything else up there, Habib," Sandrine teased. "Don't make such a big deal out of it."

"You waver just a little as you take on full corporeality, rounding that last bend," he said.

"And I always scan the bridge for you." Again, it was only saying it that she knew this was true.

Habib shook his head. Sandrine wasn't sure whether it was in agreement or disagreement. "It doesn't mean one thing or another. Don't make such a big deal out of it," he said. The dazzle of his white teeth reignited the slight tinge of lust Sandrine had been busy suppressing. She reminded herself that they'd never been lovers or even the fastest of friends, although the part of her that wished this wasn't so emerged briefly before disappearing again. She had the feeling that this shading of erotic longing always accompanied her encounters with Habib, and that, furthermore, he was right to say she shouldn't make a big deal out of it.

"I live in the city, come up to fish," he said as if patiently explaining something to a child, although he did take her hand briefly as he said it. Hugging and holding hands; these were things Habib was good at. "You live here, climb up and down an invisible mountain," he continued.

"We have what we have," she agreed.

"It is as it is meant to be, right for us," Habib said.

"It?" she asked. "In this case, what is it?"

"It may only mean that we like the same kinds of fish," Habib dissembled. They had crossed the threshold of the gift shop entering the little room with its assemblage of tinted wineglasses and cheap jewelry and knit polyester throws purchased below cost at the liquidator in nearby Stony Creek and artfully arranged by the owners to disguise this fact.

Sandrine nodded, filling two ceramic mugs with coffee. The mugs had little points all over them, like pineapples, and came in orange and green. Probably the owner Danuta had bought them at auction. Someone had unearthed a case untouched since the sixties; that was why there were so many. The mugs sat beside the coffee urn in orderly rows. Sandrine gave Habib his coffee in an orange one and watched him tear open little pink packets and dump the contents therein, one after another.

"You've got to be crazy," she said. "Aspartame. That's a neurotoxin."

"Clue?" Habib asked.

"What do you mean, clue?" Sandrine poured a single little packet of brown sugar into her coffee. The little packets were a problem too. Paper was made out of trees, even small amounts of it. Often enough they were trees from the boreal forest, the best land-based carbon sink on Earth, more effective, even, than the much vaunted Amazon rainforest.

"About the worlds," Habib said.

Sandrine ignored that. "The paper packets for sugar and aspartame are as bad as toilet paper or serviettes. Think of the energy wasted in creating such items, used once and then thrown away," she ranted. "Maybe not quite as bad, being smaller than paper towels. The cream, at least, is in a cardboard container and not in little plastic cream thingies with peelable lids."

Habib smiled. "Peelable lids?"

"I have to admit I like those," Sandrine said, pouring cream into her coffee. "All kinds of peelable lids. It's a tactile pleasure, peeling lids. Once we've cleaned the place up I know I'll find myself occasionally missing the peelable lids."

"Don't forget about the worlds."

"You keep saying that, it must be important. Oh. You mean this is one where I obsess about food and things that have gone wrong with the food system, try and help make it right?"

Habib nodded. "It's bad not just because it's wasteful and destructive to the environment but because it goes against the Creators' wishes."

"Creator? Don't you mean Allah?" Sandrine asked. She pushed open the screen door and set her coffee down on one of the little tables overlooking the canal.

"My family's secular," he shrugged. "Even in Iran they were. Part of why we left. Not so usual but who we are."

Sandrine only had a second, the one before he seated himself. She stepped forward, and enveloped Habib in a big hug. "Bismallah," she said, not sure whether she was using the greeting correctly or not. Even if she wasn't, he hugged her back. Habib, she mused not for the first time, had always been a great hugger.

"I wanted to see if I remembered more when we touched," she said, "not that you aren't huggable just for you."

What if Habib triggered her memory? Maybe part of the journey was always forgetting everything on both sides, both all memory of where she had been and all memory of what she had left behind here in the little fishing village of Brookside. A life she must eventually return to, a life that included her husband Randy.

"And?" Habib asked, seating himself.

"Nah," Sandrine said. "It was a good hug though, thanks."

"I'm glad," he said.

"Why do you think it's you I remember first, but little else?"

"Because you see me first?" Habib asked. "So that triggers your memory?"

"Seems obvious when you put it like that. So, uh," she changed the subject, "you and your folks didn't leave Iran just because of the persecution?"

"Me and my mom," he said.

She waited but he didn't say more. "Maybe you're the gatekeeper to my normal life," she ventured instead of prodding further about his family and his beliefs. If he wanted to call God the Creator, why shouldn't he? Maybe he'd borrowed the phrase from a native fishing buddy over at the nearby reserve on Highway Forty-five. Habib had a lot of friends, even in Brookside where he didn't after all live, only visiting often to fish. Maybe, Sandrine thought, it was being an immigrant that made him good at reaching out. He'd had to do it, coming to Canada from Iran with his mother, barely speaking English but needing to make friends so he could survive at school.

"Plossible," he said, putting down his already drained coffee mug. "But how?"

"Did you mean plausible or possible?" Sandrine asked, trying to be helpful.

"I like plossible," Habib said. "And anyway it's a funny question, a bit rude, like if I'd asked whether your name is Sandrine or Sardine."

"There are no sardines to fish for at Lock Eighteen," Sandrine intoned loftily, and Habib laughed.

"Why would there be?" he asked. "Sardines aren't pickerel."

"I only wanted suddenly but rather badly to use the word sardine in a sentence, it being such a wonderful word."

"Agreed," Habib agreed, chuckling.

"I see the bait shop when I'm rounding that last bend," Sandrine said, returning to their topic. "I don't remember a thing, not Danuta's name, not the blue-stemmed wineglasses, case upon pointless case of them. Sometimes Danuta is on the porch. So you're not exactly the first thing I see, not even the first person."

"The wineglasses are pretty fugly," Habib agreed, showing off his brilliant teeth again. "Maybe it's simple," he said. "Maybe I'm your gatekeeper because you can remember me, and not the other way around."

Sandrine had to think for a moment about what the other way around was. "I can remember you because you're my gatekeeper," she said. "I think it makes more sense that way. What else explains you being on the bridge every time I come down from the mountain?"

It was Habib's turn to change the subject. "What did you do up there this time?" he asked.

As ever, Sandrine couldn't remember who she'd hung out with, what she'd learned. It was beginning to dawn on her that coffee in Brookside with Habib was a necessary measure, an inexorable aspect of return. "I don't know," she answered honestly. What she did know, suddenly, was that her time was limited, that this debriefing session with Habib wouldn't last forever, that soon she would have to cross the bridge over the canal, go home to her family.

Did she and Randy have children?

Sandrine's brow furrowed; it was so hard to tell.

As if to prove her point, Habib said, "You should be going, don't you think?"

"Soon," Sandrine said. She was still thinking, still drinking her amazing direct trade coffee.

"Don't go on about the politics of food so much," Habib counseled.

"Why not?"

"Tell them about the multiplicity of worlds as well."

"It's more important?" Sandrine asked, wondering in just how many of the worlds she and Habib were good friends.

"I don't know about that. But there are fewer people who know about the worlds. Folks are catching on about the food. I feel that it's important for us to share the rarest of our knowledge, whatever it is that makes us truly unique."

"They won't believe me."

"Keep trying," he said. "It's okay if you get laughed at."

"I don't know what words to use to make them understand," she said.

"You could meditate on what they are," Habib said.

"I could," Sandrine said, "but I only know one place to do that, where getting a reliable answer is foolproof."

"Yeah, I know," he said with a smile or was it a sigh?

"Will you wait for me on the bridge?" she asked.

"When have I ever not?" Definitely a sigh, but with the faintest of smiles hidden within. Sandrine figured they knew each other too well in too many worlds to ever let their friendship go.

Eventually the sun had finished setting and she set down her drained coffee cup and crossed the bridge alone. She neared the end knowing that Habib would've gotten up and headed back to the bridge as well. Instead of crossing it he would just resume fishing in his old spot.

There were several pairs of knee-high green rubber boots on the mat, including a pair that belonged to Sandrine and one that was Habib's. They were the kind of boots people wore to go fishing or hunting, with a felt lining. It wasn't possible to buy them in the city at all. She took her own shoes off by the door as she always did. Because of this almost universal habit, Sandrine thought, country houses generally had clean floors even when inhabited almost entirely by men. The shoes Sandrine took off were new brown hikers given to her by her brother who still lived in the city and wore shoes indoors. When he visited, Anton complained his feet got cold if he took off his shoes so finally Sandrine and Mike had gone to the liquidator in Stony Creek and bought several pairs of felt slippers in different sizes and colours for their frequent guests who often included Anton and Habib. Habib, in fact, left most of his fishing gear at their house, saving the bother of carting it back and forth from the city on weekends.

Bursting through the door was disorienting, accompanied as it was by so much memory retrieval, the most important fact probably being that her husband's name wasn't Randy at all; it was Mike. Said husband was sitting at the table working on the crossword puzzle.

He looked up when Sandrine walked in and measured her with a lingering elevator glance from head to toe and toe to head. He didn't say a word but gave her the slightest of nods. What had she told Habib? That there was little if anything left to say and Mike at least seemed to understand that this was the case. He got up and put on the kettle for tea. When it was done they sat at the table and drank it, still without speaking.

CHAPTER TWO

Silent and tea drinking, Mike continued to work on the crossword. Sandrine felt the first faint waves of anxiety; just for starters she still wasn't sure whether his name was Mike or Randy. Without warning her misgivings grew from faint to furious. Sandrine had to step back and tell herself it was okay; she was just the kind of person who could look in and out of the many doors of her life. She had always done this. So many rooms in her soul, or was that self, to use the Jungian phrasing? So many memories in a house that was vast and cogent and joy-filled and realized. So many really good conversations over such amazing food, including the fresh-caught pickerel and home-cut fries that had been the first meal she and Mike had ever shared, a stone's throw from the canal in Brookside. Brookside, why was it even called that? Shouldn't it be Canalside? It was true there was a brook in Brookside; Sandrine lived on it, but the focus of the town was the marina and parks with their gazebos and the main intersection with its cafés; all had been drawn by the energy of the transdimensional gates including the populous fish populations that brought summer people up from the city.

Needing somewhere to look other than at her name-less husband, Sandrine studied their kitchen table. It had a varnished pine top and white legs. The legs, Sandrine thought, were probably not made of wood but of some kind of particle board or paste board or other wood product, basically sawdust shaped into useful shapes with the help of solvent-based glues which would off-gas carcinogens quietly, almost forever, in all the kitchens the table had already and might yet become heir to. To disguise this fact they had been at the end dipped in several coats of smooth white lacquer. The chairs were matching, with little chips out of them here and there, probably the indi-cator of why they'd ended up at the junk auction. It was supposed to look quaint, but Sandrine knew the set was probably made in a South China sweatshop, and that Mike had purchased it at the Thursday night auction in the brand new community centre in nearby Stony Creek for twenty-five dollars, instead of pay-ing the five hundred it would've cost new at Sears or Leon's or The Brick or one of their barely distinguish-able ilk.

She figured there must be a lot to rant about on this planet once you got started. Pretty much everything, in point of fact.

Be careful! She heard Habib say it, almost as if he spoke in her mind. Don't waste it! It's important, of course, the glue in the wood, but talk about the worlds. That will create more change.

Sandrine dared glancing back at Mike, or whatever his name was. He was wearing a navy blue windbreak-er and a ball cap. Almost all the country men wore ball caps. Habib, up on weekends, had taken up the green boots but not the cap. Sandrine almost wanted to get one of Mike's many caps and take it back to the bridge, put it on Habib. She wanted to stand back and observe the ways in which wearing a ball cap altered his body language.

It seemed Mike was pre-empting her plan for he got up and retrieved his green boots from the rubber mat by the door. Maybe he could tell she'd forgotten his name was actually Frank, and, in revenge for this lapse was planning to walk her back to the bridge, Habib's bridge, the same bridge where he'd found her years before, taking photographs for the Ministry of Natural Resources.

What had got them talking that day? Sandrine actually couldn't remember; it was one of the usual things like the weather. They'd gone for lunch to a fish and chips place housed in what could only be called a shack, serving pickerel caught that morning in the canal and home cut fries from locally grown Yukon Golds. She'd been impressed; it wasn't the kind of place a freelance photographer on short-term government contract usually ate at, let alone knew about, but then Mike's family hailed from this area, going back five generations.

Of course, Sandrine was local too, just not the same way Frank was local. The farm Sandrine had grown up on had been her father's country property. It was a place they went to escape the smog, roam the woods and fields for a few hours or a few days before heading back to the treadmill. She'd known her husband even back then, but he'd been peripheral, enmeshed in circles that had little draw for Sandrine. When he asked her for lunch that day on the bridge, it was almost as if they were meeting for the first time. Sandrine's memories of Mike's family returned then, if not his name. They owned farms and cottages and century brick or mid-century clapboard houses in the villages but drove old trucks and wore frayed plaid shirts, making them look poor to a city person used to measuring wealth in name brand clothes and clever phones. Not that Mike didn't care about name brand clothes. But if the brand wasn't Carhartt, he glanced askance. Why wear anything else?

Cell phones, did they even have those here?

Mike. Why did Sandrine keep calling him that when she had no idea whether or not it was even his name?

Maybe she'd been right the first time, and it was Randy. Or the last time, and it was Frank. Sandrine struggled with it again, hoped he'd give it away, and soon. Not knowing your husband's name, that was probably really bad in this world.

"So what have you been up to?" Sandrine asked at last. She felt sure that was the kind of thing you asked people in this world to whom you were close and hadn't seen for a while. Hopefully the phrasing was even right. Maybe she should've stuck to the even more taciturn "Whassup?" just to be on the safe side.

Way to go, Sardine. He's your husband. He's supposed to love you, not make you paranoid. People who love you aren't going to give you a hard time just because you asked them how they are in an idiom they're not accustomed to.

He tugged his boots on and at last spoke. "I've been trying to get Sean to give me a week off during the hunt," he said.

"What? Didn't you just take a vacation?" Sandrine asked, regretting her sharpness almost immediately. Pestering him about his vacations didn't make much sense when she'd just been away for an aeon, however long one of those even was. "So Habib can come," Mike continued. "He's never gone on the deer hunt."

"Cool. Our side of venison from last year is almost gone. Who'd you share your ticket with, I've already forgotten?"

"Mike," Mike said, which meant his name probably wasn't Mike at all but something else. Except that wasn't true. There wasn't a rule that said a Mike couldn't befriend a Mike. Sandrine remembered then that Mike, her Mike, was a supervisor at the chocolate factory in the nearby town of Stony Creek. He liked his job, mostly.

All the nebulousness made Sandrine feel irritable. Still, she drank the tea Mike had poured her, anise-hyssop she'd grown and dried herself. It was calming and restorative after the strong coffee she'd drunk at the bridge with Habib. She didn't want to talk about Mike's work or their various bills or the kids' school, any of the hallmarks of their treadmill quotidian existence she'd struggled so hard to leave behind. When had she left, anyway? Yesterday? Last month? A hundred years ago? Sandrine had a bad feeling that wasn't even a relevant question. If you wanted answers to the meaning of existence, you had to ask the right questions. She's read that somewhere, probably; it sounded altogether too clever to be something she'd come up with herself. Suzuki Roshi or Douglas Adams or Allan Watts or The Secret or The Bible. Alack, she had no idea what the right questions might be. By which criteria did one choose? It was likely they were different in each of the many worlds.

She wished suddenly and fervently that she hadn't returned to this tidy little house with its neat rows of boots and guns, even the dishes tidily stacked in a white wire strainer on the chipped counter. She needed to talk about what had been happening, and Habib was one of the few who knew how to have that conversation. He was Mike's friend too; they fished together when Habib came up from the city. Habib worked in IT with her brother at a telecom giant's head office in The Big Smoke; Sandrine and Mike had first met him at one of Anton's excellent parties.

If that was truly the case, then there were indeed cell phones here, unless she'd imported that little scenario about Anton and Habib from one of the other worlds and pasted it in. What was more irrefutable was that she and Habib always hung out when she first got back. If she didn't tell the tale of the mountain right away there was nothing to keep her from forgetting it all. She would forget most of it anyway; that was just the way things worked.

But Mike didn't know about the path up the mountain. He would fish and chat with Habib on the bridge but he didn't know about their secret lives. Mike didn't know, for instance, that Habib could see the beginning of the path up the mountain even though he had never ventured up it and possibly never would. Maybe, Sandrine thought, the time she spent up there wasn't even like time here. Maybe she was assuming. Maybe Mike knew everything.

If that was even his name. She looked at him. If only they could talk more. There was so much to complain about here in this fucked up tragic two-bit valley at the bottom of her fairy mountain. Why had she ever come back?

Because you have to, stupid. Your mind can go up there, but not your body. This was what Habib knew, fishing calmly on the bridge, watching her come and go.

Sandrine observed Mike's bony fingers handling his cup, the way he rolled himself a cigarette out of a pouch of Drum tobacco. His large clear eyes were surrounded by lashes that seemed abnormally long. The expression in his eyes was always a bit sheepish, as if he knew it was unseemly for a man to have been gifted with such spectacularly beautiful girlish eyes, at least a man who hunted and fished. On another kind of man, a professional dancer or rock musician perhaps, such eyes would've been a career maker.

But they were Mike's eyes; that was the thing of it.

Everything sucked except love. Love still held true, on any and all of the worlds. It was a hard thing to remember sometimes, a hard channel to switch back to when you were ranting.

There was a little cry from one of the bedrooms. Booted, Mike rose and traipsed down the hall and opened the door to the Sandys' bedroom. Both Sandra and Sandor got called Sandy, as Sandrine herself never did. Mike had told her that would happen but she hadn't believed him. He emerged from the bedroom cradling a sniffling Sandy, the male one. He went down the hall and pushed open the back door. He would show the child the summer stars. The stars, Sandrine suddenly knew, always had a calming effect on the boy, so wondrous Sandy went right back to sleep.

That explained the boots, Sandrine thought. Only how had Mike known the boy was about to wake up?

Maybe she'd been away so long she didn't know that Sandy always woke at exactly the same time and needed to be soothed back to sleep by the first stars. Maybe it was even the stars that woke the child.

"Maybe I came back to a different world than I left when I went up," she said when they came back in the house. Sandy was snuffling on his father's chest almost as if Mike had breasts.

"Is that even possible?" Mike asked after he'd taken the sleeping boy back to his bed.

"How is Sandy?" she asked.

"Perfect. Sandy and Sandy were both awake but are back sleeping and dreaming now," Mike said. He poured her another tea. "It's probably cold," he said. "I'll make another pot."

"I think I gave up dreaming," Sandrine said. "It seemed too dangerous, in this world."

"Not at all. Maybe," Mike said. "You changed this one just by going up and coming back."

"How do you know?"

"In the other worlds we're not together. We don't have the Sandys," he said.

She nodded; she'd seen it herself. But how had Mike? He wasn't a mountaineer. Maybe Mike had other ways of seeing things, different kinds of places he went to look at the world from an expanded perspective. "I wanted to talk about having the dream," she said, "and then reading the description of it. There is a space between them. What is it made of?"

It was the kind of thing Habib might have said, Sandrine thought, or her friend Vienna. Maybe she'd been wrong about Mike, and her negative thoughts about him were some kind of implant inserted by mischievous imps she'd run into part way down the mountain. Everyone knew the gatekeepers imps were always trying to fuck with you. She'd had more than one hair-raising encounter with them over the years or was that centuries? But sometimes the most interesting people you met on your mountaineering adventure were the ones you met halfway up or halfway down. They'd ask you for metaphorical user ID's and passwords and let you go or not depending on what your answers were. It was their job to make sure that only people who could hack it got up to the very top, which, it had to be admitted, was a place not for the faint of heart. You had to be made of sturdy stuff. The gatekeepers didn't want any wailing idiots unable to navigate so-called reality ever again based on what they'd witnessed; they didn't want that at all. Likewise, they didn't want anyone who might misuse the information they'd collected on the mountain like loosened seeds to be greedily plucked and tucked into their gathering pouches. Some might return from the mountain carrying chemical formulae, for instance, with which they might design weapons or mind control devices.

Was-His-Name-Even-Mike interrupted. "All things considered," he said, "Weapons are mind control devices."

"What?" Sandrine asked.

"All things considered, all weapons are mind control devices in the sense that they engender fear."

"Wow," Sandrine said.

"Wow, what?"

"I'd forgotten you could do that," she said.

"Erm?"

"Not erm, read my mind."

"Erming means mind reading in the language of the gatekeeper trolls halfway up the mountain," Might-Be-Mike said.

"How do you know?" she asked.

"Habib told me," he said.

"How does Habib know?"

"You told him."

Just then Sandrine saw in her mind's eye diagonals of green lozenges printed onto train upholstery long long ago, and she had to take mental time out from their conversation to reflect upon what a train it had after all been, full of memories and the moon and night. There had been camels outside the window once, sipping, or, being camels, slurping out of buckets at an oasis near Djerba. Her father had been on the train with her then, but he had gotten off a little while later, and the train had sped on through the night without him, Sandrine sitting alone in her seat, trying to converse with strangers in languages she didn't know, wishing for blankets, more money, apples, friends, all of the above. In the end falling asleep counting the lozenges, noticing their patterns, how they repeated.

She'd described it once, she remembered now, not the magical train ride itself but the strange upholstery on the seating. She'd written it up in a notebook she'd had, a notebook that might still be in a carton up in the attic above the bedroom she shared with her husband. Sandrine had been so young at the time, still a child really, twelve or so. Had the train been in Europe or in

America or in North Africa? In which notebook, either soft or hard covered, of two hundred had she written it? And why was she thinking of it now? She'd learned that often enough just the timing of certain thoughts had significance.

Sandrine felt tempted to haul a stepladder upstairs into her bedroom and unfold it there under the pink painted trapdoor to the attic. She'd climb to the top step, tea in hand. It was the kind of thing she liked to do. She'd even walked the streets of her village with a coffee mug, and not the stainless travel kind but a proper ceramic mug with daisies and ewes on it.

The first hours after getting home from the mountain were always so confusing. For instance, if there were no cell phones in this world, how did people stay in touch? Had they finally mastered telepathy? And if Mike's name wasn't Mike or Randy or Frank, what was it? Alexander? Dmitri?

None of that was the point, Sandrine mentally chided herself. She was leaping between trains of thought. She had to retrain herself to finish thoughts, or was that trains; that was part of what getting home was all about. Return always came with a massive memory loss, and really it had to. It was like being born; you had to wipe out your knowledge of the fabulous timeless spaceless omigosh infinitude from whence you'd sprung. You could never navigate through your life if you were constantly being interrupted by memories of dimensions in which your children were different ages than they were in actuality and your husband was called Rainer instead of Mike and the cell phones looked like pop tarts.

Oh stop it, Sardine, just stop it.

She was only dimly aware that at some point during this train or more accurately trains of thought she'd gotten up and walked down the hall and pushed open the bedroom door. She'd gotten the stepladder out of the bedroom closet, one capacious enough to hold such objects in addition to their meagre supply of clothing, and had opened it beneath the pink painted trapdoor in the ceiling.

The trapdoor was pink because Sandrine had once painted the walls and ceiling pink, rebelling against Mike's blues and browns and camo. It was his house; he'd inherited it along with two or three other properties both large and small and every damn wall or floor or roof or exterior wall on or in each of his houses, sheds and barns was either green or blue or brown, if not camo itself.

Sandrine stopped in mid-thought, imagining a house painted in camouflage. She smiled. It could be quite wonderful, certainly a talking point. Would she use the green and brown kind or the grey scale kind? She knew the different types of camo had different names; she just didn't know what they were. She'd painted the bedroom when Mike was away hunting, just to prove that she had some say, to prove that pink was a good colour, to prove that if Mike hated pink so much he shouldn't have married a girl; a moose would've done just fine. Mooses, after all, were brown.

Halfway up the ladder Sandrine pictured Mike's winsome moose wife and snickered. Then she climbed back down the ladder to retrieve the flashlight that always sat on her nightstand in case of a power failure; there were lots of those in the country, always had been. Mainly caused by mooses knocking over hydro poles just for the fun of it.

The truth was the pink had gotten to her too, the much and suchness of it; maybe a paler pink would've done the trick just as well, proved the point, made Mike laugh instead of groan. Predictably, they'd repainted, all except the trapdoor in the ceiling.

At the top of the ladder she pushed the trapdoor out of the way; it wasn't hinged, just a slab of wood squared a little irregularly to fit the slightly irregular square someone had long ago cut into the ceiling. She hoisted herself up and turned on the flashlight. She'd bring the box of books down, she figured, or she'd sit up there all night, opening one book after another trying to find the passage about the lozenges woven into or printed onto the train upholstery. If she was smart, once she'd found it she wouldn't slip the book, unlabeled, back into its box. She'd slap a sticky note on the offending page, or she'd get out a fine point marker and write on the cover, or she might even take the book out and carry it down the ladder to keep on her night table until it drove her crazy, until she couldn't stand it, couldn't stand even the nearby presence of this chapter from another life, all recorded here in neat cursive hailing from the days before her penmanship had gone all to hell.

She selected a yellow hardcover book from the box at random, opened it and read aloud.

"I see a beautiful board game. It is printed on an unbleached cardboard which means it is the palest brown. There is no glossy coating on the stock; the graphics are shiny, printed directly on the heavy brown card stock, mainly black and dark brown and grass green words and images.

"Over the course of a lifetime I have found that random thoughts, like dreams, can be cryptic messages from the soul, cryptic, disguised, veiled, which require only a bit of personal pondering, inspection, to parse their meaning and significance."

Not the passage about the lozenges, not at all, but maybe there was a connection nevertheless.

For instance, hadn't she just thought that?

Weird, very weird, even a little spooky.

In addition, the colours in the board game she'd described were similar to the colours of the upholstery on the train she'd written about, the passage that had sent her furtively to the attic, searching like a mouse in a grain sack for—for what?

"The café I am sitting in is like the café on 6ᵗʰ Street. That one was a basement café with nice white cups and healthy carrot bread. She would leave her apartment and walk there during the day. The clerks were supercilious. She felt her loneliness and her poverty were both recognized and snickered at, a little. She was cute enough and her thrift store coat was of good wool and a becoming cut; with a church sale silk scarf she looked quite good. And yet anyone must be able to tell that she was lonely and bored and aimless."

Sandrine heard Mike come in the room. She shut the book again, the one she'd opened more or less blindly, like a would-be traveler who sticks a pin into a globe to discover his next destination, a destination that in her case had turned out to be her Self, seeing that the endless notebooks represented a circumnavigation, a traversal of the self, in a quite literal and not just a Jungian sense.

She climbed down the ladder, clutching the little

yellow book with its descriptions of board games and cafés, if not train upholstery. At least not yet; she hadn't read through the whole thing and so couldn't be sure. She listened to her husband sit down on the bed; it must be late, even by her standards. What would she ask him once she got to the bottom of the ladder and turned around to face him?

Do you have a cell phone and if so what does it look like?

Is your name Mike or Randy?

The options were fairly pathetic, she had to admit.

She turned and looked.

The man was smiling at her, a delicious mischievous smile. She set the book down on the nightstand. She hurled herself onto the bed beside him and into his arms.

It had been a long trip home; that was for sure.

"I love you," she said because at that moment it was true.

"Of course you do," he said, embracing her in return.

"But why?" she asked. "Do you know why I love you?"

"You love me because my name is River," he said. "Men called River are deeply irresistible."

"Unless they're shallow rivers," she said. "Then they're shallowly irresistible."

River groaned, but it was in a good way. Yes, a very good way.

CHAPTER THREE

Sandrine peeked out from under the covers.

Beautiful and pale, black hair tousled, her husband River had just now elbowed her awake while getting out of bed. It was an accident, she told herself. He was just getting up for work. "Don't forget to brush your teeth," she said, which was probably worse than bitching about having been woken up.

Just shut up Sardine, she told herself, biting her pillow. He'd been asleep for seven or eight hours; why wouldn't River need a shower? What made her think he'd skip brushing his teeth on the way out the door? She lifted her head from the pillow just enough to mumble sorry and then quickly replaced it, not sure what she might say next if she didn't.

Truth was, River did like to live as if he was at the fish camp as often as he could get away with it, every day if possible. Even in the dim curtained light of dawn it was evident his teeth needed work. Even though River had dental coverage at his job, getting his teeth spit polished by a professional hygienist was something he rarely bothered with. There were better things to spend money on, such as cigarettes from the reserve with which to stain his teeth still further.

Sandrine and River lived in an area where the water wasn't fluoridated, but the purpose of fluoridation, it was well known, was not to prevent tooth decay but to keep the populace compliant. The major toothpaste manufacturers helped make sure of that, filling their products with arcane coatings, carcinogens and mind control substances that—

"Sandrine," River warned. "I can hear the fucking rant from here and you're not even talking out loud." The bedroom door shut.

"Sorry, babe," Sandrine told her pillow. "But it's true about the fluoride, as you well know." She cringed, hoping he'd only overheard the part about dentistry and not the part about his personal hygiene. Was River a telepath, she wondered, or was it the stubborn set of her chin that he'd recognized even in the blurred early light, the look that years of marriage had taught him signified an inner burn she was about to release as a toxic rant detailing everything that was wrong with this two-bit world at the bottom of her fairy mountain?

She tried to take herself in hand. It was too early to be having ruinous thoughts about the world and her husband. Part of ensuring the longevity of a relationship entailed nipping traitorous thoughts in the bud. It wasn't like River wouldn't be able to think of things Sandrine could improve about herself if he put a mind to it. But he didn't. Till this day River seemed wholeheartedly delighted to have her in his life. At the beginning he'd shown her off to his friends as if she were some kind of particularly beautiful fish he'd had the unlikely luck of landing. She was good looking and educated and from the city; everyone knew city folk were far more chic and clever than those who hailed from Brookside or even Stony Creek. Sandrine sneered inwardly contemplating this behaviour of River's; if she was feeling particularly curmudgeonly she'd grumble to herself that she wasn't a trophy fish. Did he plan to taxidermize and wall mount her? Look, guys, my sophisticated Toronto wife?

Uh, whatever, Sardine.

A showered River came back to rifle his drawers for clothes while Sandrine feigned sleep. She remembered days when she'd gotten up to make him coffee and breakfast and lunch before he left, but just now she wanted to stay under the covers, beditating. She had so many things to sort out and the Sandys were as yet blessedly quiet in their rooms down and across the hall. They might be awake, sure, but there was no reason to go and rouse them if they too were still under their respective covers picking their noses and not yet squealing for sugar encrusted pops or flakes or loops or crunches of one sort or another. Gotta git 'em young, Sandrine thought. White sugar was the first addiction, fed to the pre-school set so they could start getting in the swing of things. What after all was life in the West without a coupla addictions? Most of the time they were what got you through the day.

"It's not even true, what you think I think. We call you all citiots. Mainly because you are. I made an exception for you because you're hot," River said before shutting the bedroom door, a little more finally this time.

Sandrine looked out from under the covers; River's clothes from yesterday were strewn everywhere. Couldn't he have picked up after himself just this once?

It was strange but she couldn't remember having had quite so many pejorative thoughts about River before today. So where had they suddenly come from? Damn imps. Or maybe her eyes had been opened by her absence, the way you see everything in a new light after you've first come back from Florida. She heard the front door shut; River was gone.

Sandrine exhaled; she could figure it out later, whatever it even was. She lifted the corner of the curtain and watched him clump down the driveway to his truck, a defensive hunch to his shoulders. Mentally she blew him a guilty kiss. Her bad mood wasn't her beautiful River's fault, surely. Maybe she was just at an age when it pleased her to indulge in pissiness.

Or maybe it was part of a larger meta-exhalation, allowable now that her son was finally grown, flown away, flapping little brooms for arms as he streaked across a clear blue sky adorned with the occasional fluffy white cumulus, cumulus visible now as the sun rose.

What?

She should go out and turn off the porch light; in another hour she wouldn't even see it, glaring on the purple-black Watchman hollyhocks she'd planted beside the front door to guard the house.

Hell, maybe it was menopause.

She looked at her hands. They were young.

And even if they weren't, Sardine, menopause doesn't make you forget numbers and ages of children. That's dementia and it comes at the end, not the middle. Which you're not at yet. Get up and go down the hall. Look in the mirror. Open the kids' bedroom doors, take a good look at their babyish blonde heads.

That's heads, in plural. You have two children, not one. Don't forget you have a girl; girls don't like that, not at all.

You've had it bad before, but never this bad. The disorientation when you first get home. Maybe you should just quit going up the mountain.

Help! What world am I even in?

Who could you ask a thing like that, even?

Sandrine tossed her hair, trying hard to shake the returning image of an adult child. A child that wasn't Mike's, she was suddenly sure, but fathered by someone else, a Before-Mike. And the fact of his existence didn't cancel the Sandys' existence, not at all. Opening their door she was relieved to see they were still in bed, right where Mike had put them, although he'd been up with Sandor more than once in the night taking the little boy outside to gaze at the wheeling summer stars.

His name is River, not Mike, Sardine. This is the one fact you've managed to establish thus far. He told you last night, right before you had sex, right after you climbed down the ladder from the attic. You were up there rifling through your case of early journals, as if they'd tell you the truth of who you are. You've established your children's ages too, you've just forgotten.

Then why can I see him? He's tall and red-haired. Maybe he's Sandor, grown up, and it's the future I'm seeing.

Sandrine gently shut the kids' door and padded down the hall to the kitchen. Hopefully River had made coffee and not skipped it in favour of stopping in at Tim's. Her son stayed in her mind. He lived in Montreal, studied at Concordia. His girlfriend went to UQAM. She didn't speak much English. Her name was

Mireille. They'd come at Easter. River and Sandrine had even tried to brush up on their Français a little.

She poured coffee and sat down. She straightened crossword books and put Crayola markers and chess men back into their margarine tubs. The persistence of the image of this beautiful grown son had to have an explanation, a rational, plausible, empirically provable one.

Maybe she'd had a child before the Sandys, a boy who really had grown up and left for university. She'd briefly forgotten him because of the disorientation being so strong this time, almost like a bad concussion. It was after all less than a day since she'd gotten back.

But who was the dad, the Before-River? Someone in the city, someone she'd hooked up with when she was in her teens and had moved to Brookside in her late twenties partly to get away from. Sandrine had a brief, almost physical memory of being slapped, hard, once on the side of the head. She'd fallen to the ground.

Was that before or after she'd left him and their failed starter marriage, preferring to raise whatshisname alone? River was hubby number two, the one that lasted; the Sandys were her second set of offspring.

Problem was Sandrine knew perfectly well these strange scraps of memory were patently untrue. For one thing, she was only thirty-four; for her mystery child to be away at school, she'd had to have had him at sixteen. Physically possible but unlikely; for starters if it were true she should remember the birth, at least. Giving birth wasn't the sort of thing you forgot.

Maybe you should just stay home, Sardine. Never go up there again. It's starting to seem like it's barely worth it. Maybe you didn't decompress with Habib long enough. He's the sounding board. Or maybe, normally you stay at the café and talk longer and he tells you your husband's name and the ages and names of your children. Things he knows since he's your best friend. Things it's safer to ask him than River, because he knows about the mountain. River, while a telepath, at least now if not before, might worry you had a bad fall if you ask him his name and your childrens' names. He might, quite legitimately, insist you let him take you for x-rays and scans and things, and everyone knows how horrible wasting an entire afternoon waiting in emergency at the hospital in Stony Creek is.

Sandrine had an almost physical sense of being tugged through a porthole into here and now, her actual life, the one she really lived in. As if to prove her point, the real Sandys down the hall began to wail on cue. Sandor started, and then Sandra, across the hall, picked up the refrain.

What if for a nanosecond she'd split in two so she was part now, part later? She'd taken home a tiny snatch of the future from the mountain as comfort. Sandor would grow up, find love, pursue a higher education. All her work and sacrifice would not be in vain.

Lots of people experienced little flashes of the future, Sandrine knew. The problem she had, the problem affecting all mountaineers, was the sheer multiplicity of worlds and memories, either of them or of the future. It could be hard to tell which was which, to say the least.

For instance, why was there no accompanying image of an adult Sandra? Sandrine's stomach lurched at the possible implication. And why the stabbing glint of memory in which she'd been hit?

Just stop it, Sardine.

If the Sandys don't get up on time they'll go to school without their porridge, and then how will they be able to solve junior math problems? She supposed they could gnaw on pop tarts while she walked them to school. They could admire the colours of icing between bites. Blue and green and red eye-popping colours, pop art colours, pop goes the weasel and also the tart.

If there were no cell phones in this world how could there be pop tarts? And if her son wasn't grown up and gone off to school in Montreal, why had she just seen so clearly that he was? And if he didn't exist, then why did she miss him? Just thinking of him tied her heart in a sad little wet knot, like a handkerchief that had been cried into too often and then wrung out and then there was nowhere to put it except back in one's pocket.

The Sandys, who had politely left off while she finished her thought, resumed wailing on cue. Sandrine had to admit their timing was good. She still cared for River enough to want to spare him the morning onslaught.

"Sandy! Come for breakfast!" she yelled, crawling out of bed and sprinting down the hall. "Sandy!" she yelled again for good measure, just as she arrived in the kitchen.

It was a thing she'd sworn she'd never do, calling her two kids by the one name. Unfortunately, it happened more often than she cared to admit. River was right, she shouldn't have called them Sandor and Sandra; Trevor and Alison would've done just fine. "I promise I'll never dress them in the same outfits," she remembered telling him.

"Big help, Sandrine," he'd mocked her. "Folks don't do that with fraternal twins anyhow."

"Whatever, husband."

"It's weird because we never call you Sandy, only them."

"Do we really need to add to the confusion? I've never been a Sandy, even when I was little."

"Maybe not, but it's obvious we got the ideas for their names from your name."

"We did?" She had to admit the thought hadn't ever actually crossed her mind, but now might not be the time to admit that. The unconscious mind worked in mysterious ways; she of all people ought not to be surprised.

River had rolled his eyes. "I think we should have three more, and call them Alexandra, Sanderson and Sanford. And start calling you Sandy, in addition to them. We haven't been nearly confused enough. Not nearly as confused as we can still become if we work at it."

Is that what had happened? Had she worked too hard at becoming confused and been so successful she had trouble remembering her husband's name or whether she had another son?

She seated the Sandys at the kitchen table and poured them bowls of cereal from the health food store. The box of tiny oaten o's had been twice the price of the major grocery store brand but had promised half the sugar and only GE free grains. Stocking her fridge and her pantry with a better quality of food meant she couldn't go out for coffee as much. Sandrine sighed inwardly, already resenting this future sacrifice she was promising herself she'd make; the coffee she was talking about wasn't after all the drive-through variety but direct trade Danuta made herself in a French press. The coffee poured, Sandrine would carry her orange mug to the café's wooden porch and sit for an hour or two with Habib and watch the lock fill and empty, empty and fill. God, she could do that all day; it still seemed magic that the gates worked at all, that the containment area or pound as it was called, filled and emptied, emptied and filled, either raising or lowering cabin cruisers from one side to the next. Ta da! It was like a big metaphor for something, but Sandrine wasn't quite sure what. All she knew was that she could happily spend a lifetime trying to figure it out.

The water gates. What did they mean? For that matter, what did disliking her husband mean? What did memories of a child she'd never had mean?

There had to be someone you could ask those questions and as it turned out, there was.

"Did you forget your best friend is a professional witch?" she asked aloud.

The Sandys looked at her, giggled, and each slurped a few more o's. Sandrine called her friend.

CHAPTER FOUR

"Vienna," Sandrine asked, "Are you free at all?"

"Sure," Vienna said. "There's a party here at Hartwood tomorrow. I would have called you last week but I thought you were still up north."

"Up north?"

"Never mind," Vienna said, "wherever you were."

"I'd get a sitter and come with River but like I said I need a chance to chat."

Sandrine had given the Sandys their OJ in little plastic cups as their sippy cups were still buried somewhere in the depths of the un-emptied dishwasher. Sandra was delicately drinking her juice, setting it down and spooning little o's into her mouth from her Bunnykins bowl, then starting the whole operation over again. She seemed deeply impressed by the fact that she'd been given a grownup cup, and was determined to prove she was worthy of this new privilege.

"What I mean," Vienna said, "is I knew enough to pick up the phone instead of letting it go to voicemail, even though I didn't exactly know it was you. But that might just have been because I was hyper-focused on my new ritual and so I might have been filtering out some of the information coming through from un-related sources."

Sandrine smiled at her daughter encouragingly. "You do know what you sound like, don't you?" she asked Vienna.

"I'm talking to you, Sandrine, not my mother in law."

"Wow. Is Gayle still alive?" Sandrine asked.

"Excuse me? My mother in law is hale and hearty, calls me even though Garnet doesn't."

"Sorry if I was tactless," Sandrine apologized. "Sandor just dumped his juice into his cereal."

"Milk and juice together?" Vienna asked. "An ancient European health cure. Let him eat it."

"I'm supposed to socialize him not to do that sort of thing, aren't I?" Sandrine asked.

"Not yet. If he notices his friends aren't doing it once he's in school he'll stop right quick, let me tell you."

"OK, Vienna," Sardine laughed. "So what was the ritual for?"

"Noelle."

"Sorry, again. It's my morning for putting my foot in it."

"Never mind. As I was saying, Sandrine, I chose you for a friend long ago because if I tell you about some garden variety telepathy that occurred during my morning—" In her mind's eye, Sandrine saw her willowy friend wave her hand airily to accentuate this remark, "You're likely neither to gush nor to sneer but to take it in stride, to go with the flow. You have the necessary elevated consciousness."

Only half listening to Vienna describe knitting living herbs, Sandrine felt herself pitching into a reverie about winter parties at Hartwood. She and River used to visit when the Sandys were infants and toddlers. They'd stay overnight in one of the many upstairs bedrooms, the doors each painted a different primary colour. Maybe each door opened into a separate reality. It was the kind of thing that happened in the racist English fantasy novels she's read as a child. C.S. Lewis, Allison Uttley, Edward Eager, Edith Nesbit.

Maybe you could even tell what kind of world you were entering by the colour on the door; it seemed like the kind of amazingness Vienna might be able to pull off on a good day. Blue would signify hyperrationality, red an unpredictable passion, purple the hopeful melding of the two. The green door would open to a world populated by nature lovers, maybe a species of elf.

That's what she'd do when she got to Vienna's. She'd go upstairs and try all the doors she'd never opened, not wanting to be nosy, in all the years she'd been going there.

Maybe if she pushed through the right door, she'd find true love.

Sandrine pushed this thought away, shocked by it.

Maybe if she pushed through the right door, she'd find the lost manuscript.

What lost manuscript, Sardine?

It seemed Vienna, on the phone, was still talking about knitting herbs. "It's part of my new ritual for Noelle," she said.

"Oh," Sandrine said flatly. "You can tell me more when I get there. See you soon."

"Ciao."

She should summon up more enthusiasm, Sandrine knew. She loved her friend, and often found herself wishing Vienna could just let it go. It had been years and Vienna still blamed herself. She'd gone a little crazy, lost in her self-blame. Garnet and Eli taking off had made things worse. They'd left Vienna alone in the big rambling haunted house backing onto Consciousness, a creek which was actually called The Ouse on top and road maps. Which was pretty literary all by itself and probably didn't need any alteration on that count, Sandrine had always thought. It was the name of the river in England Virginia Woolf had drowned herself in. Still, at some point the two families had renamed the stream Consciousness, just so they could tell folks they lived on the Stream of Consciousness. It had taken, and now even some of the other people in the area, pals and neighbours and even Danuta and a couple of the other shopkeepers called it that. Sometimes on spring days when the water was high enough for a canoeist to be able to navigate the multitudinous sunken logs, she'd stuff the Sandys into life jackets and paddle from their house at the edge of Brookside to Hartwood, Vienna's house just outside Stony Creek. It made River apoplectic but Sandrine always insisted she knew her way around boats, which was true about as much as it wasn't.

It gave Sandrine pangs remembering a time when they'd all been young and happy and hopeful together. That was one thing about life; you couldn't seem to get from one end to the other without some kind of a deep burn. She wondered idly when her turn would be. She and River and the urchins had their health; they loved each other, they had enough. What had happened to Vienna and Garnet still seemed colossal, entirely unexpected, ruinous, and certainly not karmic in any easily discernible way. So what was that all about?

There were huge pastel circles on the earth in front of the house, each one a different colour. They looked as if they'd been drawn in children's sidewalk chalk. Big overlapping circles barely visible under the patchy grass. They looked old even though Sandrine had never seen them before, and she was a frequent visitor to Hartwood.

"Why?" she asked, getting out of the car to take a closer look. Sandrine knew Vienna had created the circles this morning even though they looked as if they'd faded after years of rain. Vienna knew how to use her magic to make new things that looked like they'd always been there. That wasn't their purpose, of course, just a side effect.

"It all goes back to this time I was in the city with my father," Vienna began. "Garnet stayed home with Noelle. I'd gone to help my dad paint the upstairs for his new tenant. We'd taken the dog across the street to the schoolyard to pee. Shane was a big black mongrel. He always looked really good in the winter, all black against the white. Anyway, there were huge circles in the snow that day. Did we make them or uncover them? It's a question I've asked myself a few times over the years."

"Is this a dream you're telling me?" Sandrine asked.

Vienna gave her a look as if the ultimate irrelevance of the distinction was something Sandrine, of all people, ought to understand.

"Sorry, Vienna," Sandrine said.

"It wasn't like something kids make," Vienna continued. "They looked as if they'd been made with giant cookie cutters. They were mathematically perfect overlapping circles and concentric rings. They were impossible, like snowy crop circles."

Sandrine looked at the pastel circles, their unlikely precision edged in wildflowers, yellow and orange, pink and red. St John's Wort and Evening Primrose, Red Clover and Indian Paintbrush. "Sort of like those," she said.

Vienna nodded. "The circles caught fire," she said. "My dad and I stood there watching. They burned like they had a beginning and an end, like fire snakes catching and eating their tails."

"Ouroboros," Sandrine said.

"Well, sure. I couldn't see a fuse or fuel or anything so I figured it was magic," Vienna said. "Or maybe one of those things that's really inside you. You exteriorize it, so that what's actually part of your interior landscape, your psyche, appears to be real."

"You do know that most people would have absolutely no idea what you're talking about."

"You're not most people, kiddo," Vienna said.

People had told Sandrine that before, and sometimes it had gone to her head, a little. But this time she wasn't sure. Coming from Vienna it could mean almost anything.

"It was maybe an hour later when the circles were done burning," Vienna said, "or maybe it was years. Time always goes funny at those moments."

"You step outside it. It's become totally elastic, or maybe like an accordion."

Vienna nodded. "So then we turned around and crossed the street and went back in the house. I forget which one of us made the tea."

"And?" Sandrine asked, after it seemed like enough time had passed.

"Now I understand," Vienna said, "but only now, that the burning circles were there to guide us. They were letting us know something was about to happen. They were the portals she disappeared through."

"I thought Noelle took off for the city," Sandrine said.

It was what the neighbours said, but that didn't mean it was true. Vienna had understandably fallen apart when the girl disappeared and instead of staying to help Garnet had upped and gone. What was it with men? Sandrine had wondered more than once why they couldn't handle a little heat.

Vienna nodded, fidgeting and absent. "It's too big a loss, you see," she said. "It's the kind of loss that sinks people."

Of course, lots of fifteen-year-olds took off. Normally you heard from them in a couple of days or a month. When they didn't get in touch you notified the cops. You got in contact with distant relatives you hadn't talked to in years, but maybe the girl had. Eventually you called a PI.

Of course Vienna and Garnet had done all that. Nothing.

And after awhile Garnet had gone, taking their son Eli with him.

A lot of people would stop practising magic at that point, assuming it was in some way responsible. The practising of it. The magic itself.

"That was why I made the circles on the lawn here." Vienna gestured at them tiredly. "It seemed like a reverse spell. If the circles in the city that time could warn me I was going to lose Noelle, maybe patterns of magic circles could also foretell her return. Maybe they would still work, even if they were hidden under grass instead of carved in snow, aflame. I'd try that, but . . ." her voice trailed.

"But there's no snow!" Sandrine said, hugging her friend. Anyone else and she'd have murmured a platitude, but you couldn't do that for Vienna, whose fierce eyes and aquiline nose had always, Sandrine thought, made her look a bit like a raptor. Now she was a wounded raptor, and as everyone knew, nothing bad should ever happen to eagles. They didn't take limitation well.

"Not just that," Vienna said. "I tried fire, but all I got is chalk."

"They look so old," Sandrine said, looking over her friend's shoulder. She could feel Vienna's shoulder blades under her hands. Her fingers spread, cupping them. It was an odd thing to do, but it was what her fingers wanted. Vienna didn't withdraw. Sandrine wondered who had made the fiery snow circles. Should she ask, or would that be the wrong thing to do?

"What?" Vienna asked, inching away, done with touch.

"The circles don't look like you made them today," Sandrine said. "They look decades old. Or centuries, even though that isn't really possible. There's something timeless about them, though. Almost as if they can access the future as well as the past."

Vienna toed a pink circle visible beneath patchy grass. She was wearing nice patent leather witch boots, Sandrine noticed. Burgundy. Ox-blood. Wine. What was that colour called in shoes?

"Well, that's the point," Vienna said. "To let us glimpse Noelle's return."

Which they hadn't. Unless Vienna had, and hadn't mentioned it.

Her witchy booted toe indicated two smaller interlocking circles, each a slightly different shade of aqua. "Turquoise Portholes," she added.

"Portholes?" Sandrine asked.

"Portholes, portals, round for a reason, dude," Vienna said. "I only figured it out today."

"What?"

"Excuse me?" Vienna asked. Her shoulders were hunching up. It wasn't a good sign.

"I'm not sure what you only figured out today, that's all," Sandrine said. She still wanted to know how the fiery snowy circles had gotten into the schoolyard, across from Vienna's father's house in Toronto. It didn't seem like the time to ask anymore.

Vienna gave her a faintly withering look but didn't answer, toeing a lime green portal. Her shoulders were both wide and thin. Hunching them made her look like a witch. Even though she was a witch it was disconcerting.

There were so many portals Sandrine felt a little spinny. She started walking to get a little distance, first snagging the six-pack of Corona she'd left in the car. Vienna followed her. Maybe she needed to get away from her inordinate magic too.

The gardens began just past the front yard. Among piled straw and heaps of composting manure for mulch, rows of scarlet runner beans, beets and cucumbers grew. Wild mullein grew taller than the cedar snake fence just beyond. Huge candlesticks, they bloomed yellow after Tuesday's rain. Up ahead the path wound around a pile of rusting toy tractors and an abandoned outdoor seating arrangement made of small cable spools.

"We should've used beeswax too," Vienna said, as if using beeswax might've altered the outcome.

"Never mind, Vienna," Sandrine said. "No one's perfect."

Farther along they came upon a pile that appeared to belong under the general heading of kitchen stuff. There was a surplus here of extra implements; assorted knives and spoons and ever more spatulas neatly sorted into variously coloured plastic trays. Avocado. Mustard. Burnt orange.

"Such perfidy," Vienna said. "My husband's so rich. Or is Garnet my ex-husband? Have we established that?"

"Not yet," Sandrine said. "Makes you wonder, though, why anybody ever buys anything."

"True. There's enough here to outfit several lifetimes of kitchens. Even if some of the spoons are a bit rusty or bent."

"Or melted," Sandrine said, holding up a blackened, spongy green plastic spatula. "Why didn't Garnet get rid of it? He's the one who collected all this crap in the first place, right?"

They resumed their walk, passing a circle of foxgloves. As always, Sandrine tried to imagine foxes wearing the exotic flowers on their paws, but it didn't really work.

"I don't think any of us are anywhere near healed enough to take on that question," Vienna said.

"Indeed. Are you going to build anything new this year, now that your shack's done?" Sandrine asked.

After Noelle's disappearance and Garnet's departure, Vienna, with River's help, had built a one-room cabin out of surplus and junk wood and moved into it. She still hadn't moved back into Hartwood and Sandrine wondered whether she ever would.

"A fieldstone deck," Vienna said, sidestepping a stack of screen doors. She waved her hand at an oil painting of a little girl, perched on top of the remains of a winding split rail snake fence. "For having tea with Noelle."

"Nice portrait," Sandrine said. "Was she maybe ten?"

"Eleven. When I find her she won't be able to talk," Vienna said.

Sandrine stared at Vienna. "No," she said, "no and no and no. You don't know that. Just because you're a witch doesn't give your visions any more veracity than anyone else's."

"It doesn't? I built the portals this morning so I'd catch a glimpse of her return, remember," Vienna said. "Be careful what you wish for."

"The future isn't like that," Sandrine said. "It isn't etched in stone. You're seeing a possibility, not an eventuality."

And at least in your future Noelle's alive, Sandrine also thought but didn't say.

"What's the point then?" Vienna asked, toeing a stone.

"The point of what?" Sandrine asked.

"Being a witch," Vienna said. "What would be the point of my years of study if it didn't make my clairvoyance more accurate than other peoples?"

"Lifetimes of study more likely." Sandrine's mind ka-chinged open then and she too saw the future in which an older Noelle mutely wandered the gardens of Hartwood, nimbly sidestepping the swampy spots. Here and there Garnet had assembled little boardwalks out of dismantled wooden factory pallets, going up and down the sloping hills, through the neglected orchard to the outhouse, which boasted several shelves of neatly stacked National Geographics. Through the open door Sandrine could see they had gone a little puffy from the damp.

"Indeed," Sandrine said. She took her friend's hand and squeezed it hard. Keeping hold of it she followed an orange extension cord weaving through shrubbery till they arrived. Basil and pumpkins grew out of old creamers on the little wraparound porch of the cabin, built, of course, out of scrounged wood. One of the pumpkin vines had climbed in the open front window.

"So what if I want to grow indoor pumpkins?" Vienna asked, catching Sandrine's bemused stare.

"Come inside," Sandrine said. "The download isn't finished. We need to sit down somewhere."

"I shouldn't have made so many portals," Vienna said. "What was I thinking?" She let go of Sandrine, pushed open the screen door and threw herself onto a futon couch. Shivering, she reached to the floor where last night's heap of quilts lay in a dishevelled pile. She pulled several up on top of herself.

Sandrine watched, and then she helped, smoothing the quilts and tucking her friend in. Should she make catnip tea next? Should she sit in a rickety kitchen chair from which she might fall as soon as the visions began again? She spied an upholstered armchair beside the neat stack of split kindling.

"That'll do," she said and collapsed into it, tea un-made.

Sandrine closed her eyes.

And saw night. Saw Vienna walking, making her way from one village to another, from Stony Creek to Brookside. An older Noelle walking beside her mother. They stopped for a bit to rest and hydrate and converse, except it was Vienna who was doing all the talking, Noelle nodding or shaking her head. Sandrine found herself wondering why they didn't just learn ASL. Noelle drawing then, in a black, hard covered sketchbook, night vision's delirium colouring her pastels of bright red cornstalks and purple skies. Maybe that was how she communicated now.

Vienna's witching, Sandrine knew, was long behind her. She walked without a flashlight so they could take cover in the scrub alongside the road if needed. Mother and daughter progressed through the night, until at dawn the truck stop on the highway outside Brookside opened and they could go in for bacon and eggs. Vienna would call Sandrine and she'd go meet them, taking River's truck.

"In some dreams you can remember the past of the dream world, or another part of the strange city you're in. In some dreams you see the future, including your own."

"Who said that?" Sandrine asked.

"My mother."

"This isn't a dream though. More like a shared vision."

"There's a grey area," Vienna said, "a place where dreams and visions overlap. Some people can plan to meet in dreams and then actually do it."

Sandrine saw how she'd join Vienna and Noelle and afterwards drive them home to Hartwood. Sandrine's future self loved this biweekly ritual, but nevertheless didn't mind when the snow flew and they'd put it on pause for another year. Trying to learn ASL so she could be a better conversationalist was arduous, although Sandrine felt too guilty to mention it.

We all have a future, think of that. Or at least me, Vienna and Noelle do.

Vienna opened her eyes and groaned.

"Maybe it's like residuals from the portal you made," Sandrine said. "The power sludges off, it sticks to you. Then you know things."

"Yes," Vienna said. "That could be it. Or maybe it really is a bit of info Noelle imparted telepathically from the future or wherever she is."

"Or maybe those are even the same thing, sort of."

If you two had taken better care this wouldn't have happened.

This? What do you mean, this?

I wouldn't have disappeared.

Sandrine shook her head, hard, hoping to make the weird thoughts leave her mind. Maybe Noelle actually was talking in her head, both telepathically and/or from the future, and then again, maybe she wasn't. The point being, if Sandrine was going to spend her days rowing on a sea of incontrovertible weirdness, she would have to maintain a modicum of control. If she didn't, well, the possible consequences didn't bear thinking about.

Vienna interrupted Sandrine's wool gathering. "The portals haven't taught us quite everything, not yet."

"Right," Sandrine said. "Actually, what? What do you mean?"

"Learning from and with the portals is a lifelong task," Vienna said. "One of the unsung ones that pays only in deepening joy, greater understanding."

"You sound like you're quoting," Sandrine said.

"Um," Vienna considered. "Maybe from the manual?"

"The manual?" Sandrine asked.

"For the portals," Vienna said. "Kind of like religion, only not. There's a book of notes, you see. How to take care of the portals. Like the Bible for Christianity, or the Koran or the Talmud or a book of interpretations for Tarot or Animal cards, only not. I can kind of see it a little. It's a notebook. The pages are lined and the notes are written by hand in green ballpoint cursive . . ."

"Right," Sandrine said, wondering whether she had it in a box in her attic and had just forgotten. Maybe the manual was in the same yellow hard covered book she'd found last night. The one with creamy lined pages which hadn't divulged her husband's name or, strangely enough, a description of diagonal patterns of green lozenges either printed or woven into magical train upholstery long, long ago. No, instead she'd come across a handwritten entry about a lonely young woman navel gazing at a café on Sixth Street.

Sixth Street in what city? And who had written the entry? Sandrine hadn't recognized the handwriting as her own. And she hadn't read the whole thing. Maybe there was something about the the portals on a later page.

"I used to be mad because River fucked you," she told Vienna. It was as good a time to mention it as any.

Sandrine felt exhausted by all the metaphysics. Portals and the mountain and messages from the future and/or alternate realities; all intrigued and inspired but also sapped her energy, both physically and psychically. She wanted to go home and cook and garden and play with the little ones and have sex with her husband. All the best things about corporeal existence. Maybe she and River should add kittens or puppies to the mix. Maybe some ducks. She and the Sandys could walk them to the canal for a swim.

"Not anymore?" Vienna asked.

"No," Sandrine said. "Although it took me a long time. It's because of what happened to you, I guess. If you'd been fine, I'd have stayed mad."

"How could I have been fine? Jesus, Sandrine."

"Sorry."

"And you don't really know whether or not I'm fine, even now. What someone looks like on the outside and feels like on the inside, there can be a huge disparity." Vienna swept a ragged black snake over a shoulder. "I should cut my hair, make it more like yours. I look too much like a witch this way. Some wing nut might notice and throw me down a well," she laughed. "Like my mother only she jumped."

"Your mother took her own life?" Sandrine asked. "You never told me and we've been best friends pretty much since I moved here."

"She didn't take her own life," Vienna said. "There was a portal down the well. She wanted to investigate. It's why my grandparents bought the place, was because of the portal. It was so interesting my mother never came back up. More interesting than me and my brother Dave, for example," Vienna said.

"You'll have to tell me more about her sometime," Sandrine said, instead of asking whether Vienna's mom still lived down the well. She didn't have the hour, not today. "And you know perfectly well you could stop the wing nuts before they got even halfway close."

Vienna toed an innocent pebble, almost violently. "I liked living outside," she said. It sounded almost rueful. "Even now I sometimes miss it."

"What?"

"Excuse me?"

"I meant what did you mean? What's with the non-sequitur? When did you live outside?"

"River didn't tell you?"

"River did not," Sandrine said.

"You've just forgotten," Vienna said.

"I haven't," Sandrine said. "I know I forgot about the shack for a few minutes but that was because of the proximity of your magic. It wreaks havoc on my memory, both short, haha and long term."

"It's the electromagnetic energy being so high frequency."

"The memory loss isn't permanent?" Sandrine asked.

"Not far as I know."

"You're not really helping."

"Also because that's where you and River fucked, was in the partially built shack, back when it was partially built. The Vienna living outside part no one ever told me. I'm positive."

"It was before the shack."

She's making me swallow it all over again, Sandrine thought. The bitter pill. I'm evil if I'm angry with her for letting my husband save her when she was on the skids, a rescue that included briny storm tossed sex, at least once. Even now, look at what I've got compared to her. My kids and my husband, just for starters.

Garnet hardly ever got in touch, left behind his rotting junk piles as the only reminder that he and Vienna had ever been married.

"You can look in the room if you don't believe me," Vienna said.

"The room?" Sandrine asked.

"The one with the apple green door. Pomme Verte, as we say en Français. That's where that story is."

"How can stories be in rooms?" Sandrine asked.

"How we can pluck them out of thin air, like seeing future Noelle drawing in the diner?" Vienna asked.

"Clairvoyance is common as dust. The portals you made make it stronger. Pictures sent backwards through portholes from the future," Sandrine said. "Or sidewise from one of the other worlds."

"Well, keeping pictures and stories in rooms isn't any weirder than that, if you think about it," Vienna said.

"Synchronicity. This morning when we were talking on the phone I had just that insight," Sandrine said. "That there were other realities behind the doors. What fun, I thought, to unlock and explore. Now I'm not so sure."

"Thoughts are significant," Vienna said. "It wasn't an accident, you thinking that. It was a precursor, a foreshadowing. If you look behind the doors maybe you'll find out what it was like when I lived outside. Among other things. The stories are there because that's where I put them. Or the house did." She looked in the direction of the main house with some misgivings. "It's hard to explain exactly how it works. Partly because we're dealing with magic, and it's always changing."

"That's as good a definition of magic as any. Always Changing."

Vienna nodded peremptorily. It was actually one of the things Sandrine loved most about her friend. The way their conversations could be so deep and rich and smart and layered that an amazing thought, one which another friend would offer up once a year if that, was, between her and Vienna, so usual as to be almost taken for granted, worth barely a nod before they skipped ahead to the next.

"When you go upstairs there's a hallway with different colours of doors on either side," Vienna said. "The hallway is painted white and each door is a different bright colour. Red, green, blue, yellow, purple. Primaries, secondaries."

"I know what your upstairs looks like. River and I stayed in Red at your parties, more than once. It was just a bedroom."

"Macintosh you mean."

"They all have apple names?"

"I think they do now, I'm not totally sure. Didn't use to. It's not important, really. Mystery number one," Vienna said, "is that sometimes they're bedrooms, sometimes they're stories. Mystery number two is that there are far too many doors off that hall. In spite of its tower, Hartwood isn't a very big house, not from the outside."

"True," Sandrine said. "It's like a gothic mansion only it's not a mansion."

"I don't know how the house does it," Vienna said.

Sandrine wondered whether Vienna and River had built the cabin so she could get away from Hartwood. "Why didn't you ask me to help you build the shack too?" she asked.

"I think I did," Vienna said. "But you were busy being mad. I've got to start on another one for Noelle."

"The tiny house approach, saves on taxes. But Noelle can live in the big house."

"Maybe she left because of something in the big house."

"Could be," Sandrine said. "For example, the fact that there's a story world behind every bedroom door in the upstairs hall which is, and this is comparatively minor beside the other, too long to fit inside a medium sized house."

"Comparatively."

"A second shack is a lot of work even if that's true. You don't know whether what we saw is real," Sandrine said.

"Excuse me? I don't know whether it's real that my daughter is coming home?"

"Sorry. I know it's an image I shouldn't doubt. Not from you, not at this point."

"I worked for days on the portals," Vienna said. "We saw the pictures hurtling through them to land, unmistakably fragile and beautiful, at our feet."

"But there are still a million futures at any given time. A million possible futures. In spite of what we saw. I'm almost certain."

"Almost being the operative word. You're just trying to get out of helping me. I can drive over to River's factory and ask them for old pallets."

Was there an under-layer of threat? Did Vienna mean she planned to fuck River and build a shack both? The dual activity had worked so well last time. "It's not his factory, he just works there," Sandrine said.

"You know what I mean," Vienna growled. "And I'll betcha anything he does own it, or part of it. Pretending he's a supervisor is just cover. Like everything else about River. Broken down trucks, bad teeth. Have you ever asked to see his complete financial records, Sandrine?"

"Don't get stuck. If you obsess you'll make that reality more likely to adhere."

"Which reality? The one where she comes back? Why wouldn't I want that one to adhere? And adhere to what? Define your terms."

"Shut up, Vienna, you know what I mean. The one where she comes back mute."

Telling Vienna to shut up might have been an error in judgement. It had its source in an earlier time, one in which there had been been picnics, swims and camaraderie.

"Maybe Noelle likes being mute in the future," Vienna growled. "Maybe she likes drawing more than she ever liked talking. Maybe it's a choice. Did you ever think of that?"

"It's a guilt projection. You think you did something bad, so something bad has to happen in return. Most of people's ideas about karmic retribution are guilt projections. The universe doesn't care what we did, at least not much. It wants us to be happy. It knows we're fuck-ups and forgives us. Anyway, what do you think you deserve retribution for?"

"Putting story worlds in the upstairs bedrooms. That much magic attracts the dark. Sleeping with your husband."

"Those were both after, not before Noelle disappeared."

"How can you be so sure?"

Oh fuck me, Sandrine thought. Had Vienna been sleeping with River all along? That would cast a shadow on their sunshine dappled memories, playing in rowboats on the stream, alongside their friends the river otters and snapping turtles. Not that it wasn't understandable. River being so hot. Garnet being so distant. "Maybe you should do what you were going to do before I got here. Finish your potholes."

"Excuse me?" Vienna's bushy, but not quite Frida-esque, eyebrows flew skyward. Her eyebrows had been on fleek long before the term was coined.

"Portholes, portals," Sandrine said. "Whatever they are."

"You said potholes. In a sarcastic tone."

"Ironic, not sarcastic."

Vienna advanced menacingly, as if their recent bout of sisterly hand-holding was something they needed to put behind them. Sandrine met her gaze. Saw the look in Vienna's mad tired eyes. The witch was capable of anything, in her current state.

Sandrine turned and ran, cornering a stand of cedar.

When she knew for sure Vienna wasn't following she slowed enough to walk a beautifully mown path between junk piles. She came across a wooden skid where someone had done a little sorting. A coffee can for screws, one for nails, a plastic tray of hammers and other hand tools. Beyond the junk piles, the cabin's eaves were visible again, peeking beyond a tamarack, whose branches grandly swept the ground—sort of like Vienna's hair, at least when she was sitting down. Sandrine stared at the roof, exasperated. She had gotten completely turned around if she was heading back towards the shack. Or maybe it was an electro-magnetic disturbance caused by Hartwood itself, the house with a personality, and not always a nice one either. Or the potholes. Whatever they were.

"The shack Vienna fucked my husband in," Sandrine said aloud. It shocked her a little, doing that. She wasn't usually the sort of person who raved or swore about things out loud, even quietly. That was more Vienna's style.

Stop it, Sardine. You know where this leads.

Behind her, twigs snapped. Sandrine had been fol-lowed after all. She turned to stare at her mad friend. Portal energy torsioned off Vienna in wretched, angry swirls. Sandrine felt out of her league. Chamomile tea wasn't going to help with this.

"Why don't you go up to Hartwood?" Vienna asked in a voice so hard it glittered. "You can climb the stairs to the second floor where too many doors are painted too many colours."

Maybe it was a voice that Sandrine found shock-ing, but which River had heard a million times, back when Vienna camped out in the swamp. A spooky voice he had wanted, badly, to rescue. Sandrine won-dered about that. There was nothing helpless about this aspect of Vienna.

"Push open door number two, Pomme Verte," Vienna continued. "Then maybe you'll find out what actually happened."

"Maybe I'll find out more than I want," Sandrine said.

"Quite possibly. But what if you find true love?" Vienna asked.

"True love is overrated." Sandrine said.

"You only say that because you have it. How about the lost manuscript, then?"

"What lost manuscript?"

"Only one way to find out."

CHAPTER FIVE

Sandrine snuck through the house called Hartwood listening to it breathe and sigh at every interval. She turned corners and climbed stairs and worried the witch Vienna was behind her, had singled her out with malicious intent. But the witch was her best friend after all and had advised in the first place that she come from the guest cabin up to the main house and climb the white painted servants' stairs off the kitchen and, on the second floor, examine the double row of brightly painted bedroom doors, attempting to decipher which one drew her most.

Which door should she open? Sandrine had to decide quickly; if she stood here dithering she might change her mind and clatter back down the stairs and hitchhike home to Brookside, her husband River and their little twins the Sandys.

Seizing her initial whim, she pushed open the green door, called Pomme Verte after its colour which was precisely that of a Granny Smith. It was also the door the witch had recommended she pass through, a fact which gave Sandrine a bit of a sinking feeling, for you never knew, not really. Not with Vienna, even before she'd become ill.

However, once inside there was no turning back. Sandrine felt snatched by the storytelling power of the room inside the door, by its purpose and drive. It was as if the witch's story itself sat her down on a little wooden bench and made her watch, for participating was something she couldn't do; this was not like a dream.

The little wooden bench was none too comfortable but that didn't matter so much for the story was as gripping, absorbing and ensconcing as any story could be.

Once inside the door, just for starters, Sandrine saw how it was true: Vienna really had lived at the bottom of the gardens on Vine Street. Lawns and flower borders and vegetable patches gave way to woods, mostly cedar and various species of willow for it was damp. Nature's natural cycle seemed altered there, for the ground was in places knee deep in broken sticks, and littered with the arms of dead trees.

It was a sorry sight, but a sorrier feeling, for in the very next moment, Sandrine turned into Vienna and became a participant.

Don't judge until you've worn another woman's shoes, or however it goes, Sandrine told herself in the split second before her friend's personality took over. In that brief second she wondered whether she'd ever get herself back, or whether the shift in perspective would be permanent, and from now on she'd live out her life as if she were her friend.

And if that was the case, was Vienna now forever her? Had they traded?

Before she lost the last dribble of her Sandrine-ness, she reminded herself the whole mess was patently impossible.

Except that with Vienna, you never knew.

Vienna was a witch, after all. Even her house had a personality all its own, and not always a nice one either.

It was March and I piled sticks and some old half rotten clothes into a big heap; the village teenagers might come to have a bonfire now that spring was in the air. No one else came down much, so the few paths were overgrown. They were brambly and hard to struggle through, and decorated with takeout containers, beer bottles both whole and dangerously broken, and Styrofoam, both in cup and slab and pellet form.

The streets and driveways of the town were swept clean often, the lawns sprayed and weeded and raked and mowed, but no one cleaned up the owner-less woods, unless the witch did it, meaning me. I didn't actually hear what people said, but I could guess. They thought I was stupid enough to believe that if I cleaned up after them they'd give my daughter back. As if.

Noelle wasn't dead. I was sure of that. I'd have felt it if the girl was dead, just as I'd have felt it if Garnet or Eli had died. But I knew my family was still alive. I just didn't have them near me anymore, the way they were supposed to be.

Early spring runoff filled the lowland gully beyond the fallen trees and piles of sticks. I gathered cans and bottles, disconcerted as ever by how many had once contained hard liquor of all sorts. I also mumbled. I knew it didn't help my reputation much. When had

I begun? I rarely even left the woods anymore except early on Thursday mornings to fill the town's recycling bins. Why, I often wondered, was it better to dump garbage off the bridge at night than to sort it into bins? Why was that so hard? But the townsfolk couldn't, wouldn't, didn't.

I knew that even before dawn on Sundays they made an opposite trek to my own. They went out, also with sacks, to the bridge across town and tossed their old pillows, used condoms, empty pill bottles, pornography, vomit stained sleeping bags, single shoes and even used toilet paper into the gully. They treated the ditch beneath the bridge as an impromptu landfill in the middle of town. And who could blame them? After all, green, orange and clear garbage bags hurled on top of one another made such a nice sound: a kind of sliding squishing ker-thunk.

The witch, they seemed to think, would deal with it. After all, I always had.

In the morning, after their midnight purges, they could go to church and gossip about how I filled my days weaving disgusting things out of old string I scavenged. This, at least, was true.

I wove webs out of the dirty old string, and hung them from the trees. They were like things spiders on LSD might have made, and there were more each month. Each intricate piece of webbing took me several painstaking hours to make. I was pretty sure it was because of my spider webs that my neighbours could face the day telling themselves they were nice clean decent people. I would have if I could have, but it wasn't actually possible for me to stop making them. Like the decade-long cigarette habit I'd finally given up when I got pregnant with Noelle, they were a compulsion.

Surreptitiously, I tipped my sacks of cans and bottles into the big blue plastic boxes at the end of the lane. When I was done I saw a woman approaching me. I'd seen her before. She too made the rounds early on Thursday mornings, combing the streets for things she might drag home to stock her weekend yard sales.

"Looks like rain," the woman said, when she got close enough. It was unusual for her to speak. Usually we just nodded when we crossed paths.

"Have much luck today?" I asked.

"Some old shirts, and two nice lamp stands." She gestured at the lamps, missing shades.

I'd been up on my vintage housewares once, and knew the mid-century lamps would garner a hundred dollars each at a trendy retro boutique in the city. But how would the woman get to the city if she had no vehicle? And how much would the store owner give her for the lamps? If she only got enough for gas and lunch it wouldn't be worth it, beyond being a free trip to The Big Smoke, which, admittedly, counted for something.

"The lamps are nice," I said. The stands were realistically glazed ceramic ducks, and there didn't seem to be any chips out of them.

"Do you want to buy them?"

"No," I said. We'd already spoken more than we ever had. Talking to another person instead of to myself was actually quite hard.

"I guessed not," the woman said, laughing.

Was there a touch of derision in her laugh? I couldn't be sure. "Why's that?" I asked.

"Where would you plug them in?" she asked.

"Excuse me?"

"They say you sleep under a pile of odds and ends," she said. "Under a heap of other people's garbage and sticks." The ragpicker looked at me. I waited for the verbal spasm of hatred I felt sure must be coming next, either from myself or from the woman. But we just kept looking at each other, and finally I pointed at the lamps and said, "You'll get twenty or thirty dollars apiece for them when the cottagers open up on the May long weekend."

The woman beamed, looking immensely pleased. I glanced at the black hooded sweatshirt draped over her arm. It looked quite new. "My daughter would've liked that," I said. I didn't want to end the conversation, challenging as it was. I thought it might be the first real one I'd had in years.

The woman stared. "You had a family once, didn't you?" she asked.

"I still have them," I said. "They're just not here."

"Your daughter was very bad," the woman said. "She sold drugs at the high school and was killed by the bikers who supplied her when she didn't pay. They cut up her body and distributed it in many places, so they could never be caught."

I figured then the woman had been poor and isolated for so long it had driven her crazy, and forgave her this new assault.

"That was Paul Hubert," I corrected. "I heard that story too. Everyone knows that story. Poor Paul. Imagine how his mother must have felt. What was her name again?"

"Aimée."

"Yes," I said. "Why didn't Aimée teach him to love himself? If he'd loved himself, he wouldn't have turned to drugs, either the buying and selling or the doing."

"You don't know that for sure. A lot of the kids around here get into drugs."

"Yes, but I think no one had taught her either. If the mothers were cared for and shown respect, we'd all be in so much better shape."

This last came out of the witch wisdom my own mother Roo had taught me. I hadn't said anything like it in over a year and was a little surprised. After Noelle's disappearance, what had any of it mattered? If my magic hadn't been able to protect my daughter, wasn't it worse than useless?

The woman looked startled. "They said you couldn't even really talk anymore," she said.

"I couldn't," I said. "But I had to defend Noelle. Usually I don't hear the rumours. Mostly no one says them to my face. This is the most I've talked in months, maybe years."

"It was all so long ago," the woman said, memory dawning on her creased face, and I didn't know whether she was referring to Noelle, or to Paul Hubert, or to her own demise. "We're not any of us as young as we used to be," she continued, peering at me. She looked familiar, as if we'd once sat on committees together. We'd baked for the same fundraisers, surely. "Frances," she said, stretching out her hand. "Frances Fish."

Ah, the minister's wife. What had happened to her? I must have heard, and then forgotten, just as Frances had mistaken Noelle's story for Paul Hubert's. Even in a small town, memory was fickle.

What about me? Did I really sleep under sticks? What my life had become, it sure wasn't what I'd planned. I shook Frances's hand. "Vienna Straw."

"I know who you are, Vienna. You had the most beautiful gardens, flowers and vegetables both. You were a good herbalist and you always looked elegant."

"I was just born with skinny genes, is all. And I was good at putting together outfits from thrift stores. If I had money for new clothes I gave it to Noelle."

"It was always so important to them," Frances said, "the right kind of sneakers and jeans at school."

"Yes."

Frances smiled. She leaned forward a little as if she was thinking about hugging me, but then she backed off. I don't think I flinched, but neither of us was ready to go that far, not yet. We parted, and the next Thursday Frances wasn't out, nor the next. I went back to piling sticks and talking to myself.

"The paths through the cedars are all grown over with brambles and garbage. The slabs of Styrofoam and piles of old shoes replicate at night, so that in the morning there are even more. Why always this bleak-blackbadness, inconsolable beyond hope at the core, at the bottom, collecting at the fallen logs. The beads of dirty Styrofoam, disintegrating. They make me feel so ashamed."

There were moments I thought I might die under the weight of it. But I couldn't; what if my daughter came back and I wasn't there?

"Maybe they'll give Noelle back if I take their garbage as well as my own. Heaping it into a higher and higher mound every night after spending hours and hours and hours collecting it. Afterwards burrowing beneath it to sleep, in spite of it smelling rather badly. There, I've just admitted it, even to myself. I'm looking for my daughter's body," I muttered, still piling sticks. I'd just misplaced Noelle somewhere. "My daughter isn't dead, only mad or missing," I said. "Maybe she's not out here at all. I bet they've got her in a basement somewhere."

But it was me who was mad and missing, and not Noelle at all. I didn't know that then, and it was a hard thing for me to learn. I couldn't have done it without my friend River's help.

The week after that the geese were flying overhead in pairs, looking for nesting spots, just as Garnet and I had come back to the old place in Stony Creek, wanting a quiet pretty place to raise our kids. The geese honked at me derisively, so I built an actual lean-to out of deadfall and Styrofoam instead of burrowing under my shame piles to sleep. I tried not to talk to myself so much. My conversation with Sally Fish had been so short, and was now weeks old, but it had still reminded me of the difference between near total isolation and a smidgen of companionship. My husband had often made fun of my mumbling. I'd done it even when he was still around. But mumbling to a person doesn't get you called crazy; it's just a little rude.

But with Garnet gone so was my cover.

I unwound string from a tangle of sticks and sat down on a pile of other sticks. I began to make a spider web, part God's eye, part dream catcher. I arranged little sticks into a star and wound string around their central meeting place to hold it secure, and then I began weaving the string beneath the spokes, moving towards the outside. I'd try to create and follow a pattern but usually broke with it before I was done, careening into a no man's land of haphazard, mad crochet.

When they were finished my creations unfortunately never seemed beautiful and powerful as I'd intended but, rather, pathetic and lonely. Nevertheless on sunny days when there was a breeze the swamp at the edge of the village became my private gallery, the little bits of broken bottle glass I'd woven among my crazy wheels' spokes glinting like anxious dancing fairies.

I survived the spring's windiest gale in my makeshift lean-to. My shelter looked a little like an igloo from a distance, the water rounded white slabs piled into circular walls. The Styrofoam had good insulation value.

The geese flew back and forth several times each day, and at last I broke down and cried, missing my husband so badly I couldn't give the pain a name. Geese mated for life.

I should've followed Garnet. He actually did ask me to go with him, but I didn't. I don't tell people that. Not even Sandrine or River. It's not that I want a pity party. It's that I couldn't go with him. I had to stay in case Noelle came back.

I kept busy knitting and crocheting, and gathering sticks to wrap my mad weaving around. That was a project in itself. They had to be straight, and their entire length the same circumference, more or less, and they had to be of a sturdy enough wood not to snap when I started winding string onto them. And every day I wondered why my burrowing and my knitting didn't coerce the townsfolk or the spirits or gods to give Noelle back. My daughter catchers were witchy magic, after all. They were supposed to work.

I heard Garnet opened a shop selling collectibles. He knew most of his facts and would be able to back up each piece of begged or borrowed or stolen or scavenged bit of merchandise with a story, quite likely to be true. Twice I found rusted old guns in the swamp, detritus of long-forgotten hunts or maybe even skirmishes. I put them away in a drawer for my husband. I would gift them to him should he ever pass back through.

Sometimes as I cleaned the forest I'd notice I was talking to my daughter. When that happened I would start to cry. Noelle and I had been close. We'd liked the same things: poetry and painting and witching.

It gets you every time, that witching.

We should've chosen different professions. At one time or another in her life a witch will always have stones thrown at her. My own mother Roo, also a witch, told me via telepathy, trying to herd me to a gentler occupation. But Roo spent my entire life living at the bottom of the well, and I've come to distrust her advice because of it. In fact, she still lives down there, and she hasn't once mentioned Noelle's disappearance. Maybe Roo can't really talk anymore either. Either way, for me the witching is the gentlest task I know, and the most necessary. I turned my back on my own mother's words, my own mother's tears, convinced that Noelle and I could together change the world's view of what a witch was.

Still, I longed for the storied days of yore that had preceded even Roo's time, the days when witches were well paid and cared for with kindness and invited to good parties and not forgotten but necessary and ostracized in the ragged woods at the bottom of the gardens. Roo was right, of course, except that I myself managed to avoid the stoning my entire life, and the gossip I'd inured myself against.

But all that was before they stoned Noelle for practicing magic.

After which she disappeared.

Or is that during? Maybe her magic was to disappear.

She never came back, or I haven't discovered in which basement they're keeping her.

Even from down her well my mother Roo was able to teach me how clear intent poured into the creation of an object will amplify its power to heal, or for that matter to harm. Roo's teachings have been mainly telepathic. Because of it, they're not verifiable. I could even be making them up, imagining a mother where I actually have none, or maybe, by now, a waterlogged blob, only barely sentient.

We don't communicate much anymore. Since everything happened I have stopped asking my mother for help. I have been afraid Roo would be disappointed in me.

There are thirty or forty spider webs strung here and there. My daughter catchers are not just unsuccessful but also disturbing. No wonder not even the dog walkers come down much anymore.

Filled with chagrin at this realization, I wandered the woods with a new purpose, ostensibly to find and detach and burn all my creepy hanging things. I found and bagged six, and where I thought I'd hung the seventh, I found a young man instead, stuffing it into his pocket. He looked to be maybe eighteen, although I'm not good at guessing ages.

"Why do you want that?" I asked.

"Want what?" he asked, his hand covering the bulge in his pocket.

"My spider web," I said. "I made it."

"Noelle made them," he said. "They bring luck in love."

"How could Noelle make them if she's gone?"

"Maybe she's a ghost," the young man offered.

Was he cruel or just insensitive? I wasn't sure. "No-o," I stuttered, "they've got her and they won't give her back. If I can just figure out which basement they've got her in I could break in."

I trailed off. You aren't really crazy if you know what you sound like, right?

"You look cold," the boy said. "Come to the fire for tea?"

"Sure."

There were five or seven of them, sitting on logs and stumps and broken chairs arranged around one of my stick and garbage piles which they'd set alight. They made tea in an old kettle and gave me some in a chipped cup. They poured a little rum in their own and asked me if I wanted any. I didn't refuse.

"Just don't break the bottles, OK?" I asked. "I cut my fingers when I clean up down here."

"I wouldn't," the boy said. "What's your name?"

"Vienna. You?"

"Theo."

"Hello, Noelle's mom," Theo said.

"Why aren't you afraid of me?" I asked Theo. "Most everyone else is."

"Because you're Noelle's mother. Noelle is magic so you must be too."

"But I'm evil. She must have been evil too, or they wouldn't have stoned her." It was only saying it aloud that made me realize some tiny part of me believed it was true.

"You're not evil! You're just sad because of what happened to Noelle."

What had happened to Noelle? What if Theo and the other kids knew something I didn't?

"It could happen to anyone," Theo continued. "But don't stop making those weird string things. They're infallible."

"You young people collect the charms because you want someone to love you, yes?" I asked, struggling to understand.

"Yes," Theo said, "but not just anyone. They work to make someone in particular love you, if that's what you want."

Well, who didn't want that?

I love my best friends Sandrine and River and their little ones Sandra and Sandor. That family is my mainstay, keeping me safe and sane when everything has been rent asunder. I love Garnet and Eli and Noelle, even though they are gone. I loved my father. I still feel connected even though he crossed over years ago, a month after our fire circle ceremony. I love my brother. Dave lives in B.C., and neither of us has the funds to make the trip every year. Sometimes more than a few go by before we see each other. It makes me sad when I think about it, but sometimes I forget to even do that.

"You can't control people," I told Theo, "even by magic. Especially by magic. That's not what magic is for. Although it's a temptation more magicians and witches have succumbed to over the ages than resisted. I should know."

There was something about Theo that inspired me to speak in long complete sentences. Maybe it was just mutual compassion. He seemed like such a nice kid I was overcome by the desire to help him.

"My mother never loved me," he said. His tone was more matter of fact than self-pitying, but I could still tell it had been hard for him to say.

"I know all about mothers who can't seem to love. My mother gave birth to me whilst submerged and never held me in her arms," I said. "She had to let me float to the top of course, so I could breathe, as I don't have gills like she does. Or whatever it is that enables her to breathe down there. Roo still lives in the well between my house and barn. I'll bet yours loves you more than you know. Weird as it seems, a lot of people have more trouble expressing love than anger." I spoke as gently as I could, but left a thread of growl at the bottom. I wanted the child to understand I wasn't just a pathetic freak. I still had a little witchy power, and might be able to help him in his situation because of it.

"Maybe you should go up to the house one day and call down to see if she answers," Theo said.

"I haven't been back to the main house in over a year. I might think she doesn't have any answers for me anymore but when was the last time I asked?"

"My mother," Theo said. He glanced haplessly at a girl sitting on a stump by the fire. She smiled encouragingly, pulling on one of her long braids, dyed to match the black in her thigh-high striped socks. "I can't really blame her too much because we live in such different worlds. In her own way she probably does the best she can. All the same I miss her. I call to her on those days when you feel you could almost walk through walls."

"I know just the ones," I said. "When the veils are thinnest."

"Her name's Sandrine," Theo said.

"Fuck me!" I exclaimed.

Theo looked nonplussed, to say the least. His watery blue eyes swam behind spectacles.

"Sorry, dude," I said. "She's my best friend. You're right, she lives in another dimension."

"Literally?"

I nodded. "I've never heard of anything like that before, ever. I'll try and think of something." I meant it, too. How had Sandrine's son ended up living in a different dimension from the rest of us? It beat all.

"Can you give her something for me?" Theo asked.

"Of course. What is it?"

"A notebook. She's been looking for it." He handed me a green hard-backed journal.

I put it in the pocket of my coat. I figured it was more likely I'd be wearing the coat when I visited Sandrine in her dimension than not. It most definitely wouldn't do any good sitting on a shelf in my Styrofoam igloo.

"I love you, Theo," I said, because I did. Of all of us, it struck me he was the least selfish.

He blinked behind his spectacles, and smiled a little smile. "Please don't forget to give it to my mom," he said.

"The love catchers have worked for lots of us," Theo's friend said, so I let him keep the one he'd found. Surely each and every one of us is in need of a little more love.

I smiled to myself, thinking of my mother. Instead of nursing me underwater which might have drowned me she'd given me the gentlest of shoves so that I'd rise to the surface in time to take my first breath. In spite of our circumstances, Roo and I had managed to develop and maintain fairly reliable telepathic communication. That was quite a feat in itself, at least if our conversations had veracity and weren't just a byproduct of my overactive imagination. Like mental gelatin, say, or pressboard.

I ought to be proud of that, maybe even proud enough to go up to the house, if only just to take a look around. I could call down the well, send Roo greetings.

When was the last time I did that? Was it months ago, or years?

If I went in the main house I wouldn't have to sweep or anything. I wouldn't have to do the bills or wash dishes or organize dinner parties. I wouldn't have to have sex with Garnet for the relationship's sake even when I didn't totally feel like it, because Garnet was gone. Did I really want him to come back? He might want me to start up with the sweeping and dinner parties all over again, and we know how that ended last time.

I could just sit on the back stairs behind the kitchen instead, and think. Halfway up, halfway down, neither upstairs nor downstairs, neither here nor there. Goddess, I was starting to sound like Sandrine when she yarked on about her mountain. And maybe because of it I was starting to understand her more.

Entertaining that possibility I fell asleep, the fire and the rum so warm. When I woke the moon had risen and the young people were gone. On the way back to my Styrofoam igloo I glimpsed a silvery sliver of water beneath a heap of deadfall. Investigating further, I foolishly stepped in, and then lost my balance and fell, for the bottom was muck. Shocked, I righted myself, the icy April water well past my knees. I grasped for a hanging tree branch but it snapped off in my hand. What did I expect from a Manitoba Maple? What is the point of those uselessly brittle trees, anyhow? After that I was left with tough frozen grass to grasp and haul myself out by. It worked, but not before I raised my heart rate thinking I was done for.

Nothing like thinking you're about to go into cardiac arrest to make you appreciate life.

Had there always been a creek here? It was as if I'd forgotten its existence, but how could that be? It was so full of deadfall and garbage it was almost entirely obliterated from sight, but that didn't account for its absence from my mind.

I saw another daughter catcher then, hanging from a branch just out of reach, almost as if it had been detached and re-hung by the wind. I hiked my skirt in spite of its wet weight and shinnied up the tree. I knew the burst of adrenalin that had gotten me out of the creek below wouldn't last long and that once it was gone I'd be shaky and ready to fall in the water and die of hypothermia all over again. Gritting my teeth, I snapped off a big Manitoba branch that was in my way and tore the vagrant daughter catcher down. How had I gotten it up there in the first place? It must have been a nicer day, a day when climbing half dead trees didn't seem like a subtly suicidal act.

Like smoking, say.

There was beautiful magic in my webs, including the yearning I felt for Noelle.

Maybe it was even my woven longing that helped the kids find the love they craved. I put the daughter catcher in my pocket and clambered out of the tree. Maybe it would work for me too.

On the way home I remembered the creek. One spring when it flooded its banks Eli, Noelle and Sandrine and I had slipped into the water and been pulled around two bends until we got to the place where several fallen trees slowed the current. Screaming and laughing, the four of us, laughing because of the speed and fierceness of the ride, screaming because the water was still icy with melt off. Everything so green. Each spring it felt like that, as if a winter of starvation was being assuaged. I remember thinking that day had been so much better than the expensive asphalt paved fair. A better thrill, and free. My family and friends and I had looked into each other's eyes, wide with excitement, barely believing anything could be so wonderful. And then done it again.

How could I have forgotten the creek? It must have been my trauma.

But it seemed not only me but everyone in the village had forgotten.

When I got home I was appalled by my stick and Styrofoam shelter. I'd never really seen how I lived before now. What if the spiderweb I held in my hand had helped me wake up? If its magic was to draw love, that could include self-love, which had been my prescription for poor dead Paul Hubert.

I crawled into my igloo and my nest of sleeping bags. Where had they come from? I must have dragged them down from Hartwood at some point.

In the morning I walked the paths, hoping the young people would be at their fire circle and invite me for tea. But there was only cold ash and I understood it was a school day. Maybe they'd come back later.

The goose and her husband flew overhead, honking. They were taking a long time deciding where to build, or else they just wanted to extend their weeks of dinners out and movies and sex, before the long work of raising a family began.

I wished again my man hadn't left. I wished Garnet had stayed behind and helped me look for our daughter. I wished he'd believed that our love could find a way. I had often secretly felt there was a streak of weakness in Garnet, an inability to hold on, hold out. He'd always worried about what people thought more than I did. If I'd been sure he was standing beside me it would've been easier to speak.

What might I have said? Something like this:

"Noelle was just letting her hair down, letting off steam. Her magic was beautiful. You were afraid of it because you don't like magic. You don't like my magic either, but it's quieter so it's easier to ignore. My mother Roo is the quietest of all. Each generation the witches get a little louder. We're starting to come out of our collective shells. One day we'll be back to the way we were in days of yore and then everything will be right with the world. Even with your worlds."

I hadn't actually known that's what I would have said until that moment.

I've always worried I should've spoken before the stoning even happened. When I first felt it coming I might have said not just the above but also something like this:

"Noelle's a little frisky, it's true, but great care must be taken of the free-spirited; they teach us all that joy is still possible. To judge them is to judge ourselves. We'd do better to imitate than to decry. Maybe if you had more real fun you'd throw less icky pornography off the bridge at night."

But I hadn't. Or if I had, I hadn't said it enough. Or if I had said it enough, it hadn't made enough of a difference. They'd still stoned Noelle. She'd still gone mad or missing or both.

Hindsight. There's nothing like it for putting words in people's mouths, including, it seems, mine.

I decided to investigate the missing creek.

At which point Sandrine was once again manipulated and transformed by what or whoever managed the realities behind the coloured doors until she wasn't Vienna anymore; instead she was watching her.

Poor Vienna, poking at the secret creek with a stick, her long hair matted, her cloak in rags. The image began to waver and Sandrine worried she was about to throw up. She didn't, thankfully, but she felt herself being spit out of the green door, as if it were a mouth and she a lemon pit.

When she gathered enough of her wits about her Sandrine discovered she was lying on the floor in the upstairs hall at Hartwood. She didn't move right away, struggling to process. What had just happened? As an experience, going behind the green door had been discombobulating, but also so entrancing she wanted to push open one door after another, to experience what or who lay behind each. Sandrine looked closely at her hands. She almost expected them to vanish at the wrist, as if they were still poking through a membrane into an adjacent dimension. Maybe that would actually happen if she reopened the green door and pushed only her hands into the space that lay beyond, but she was too dizzy to try it.

Maybe I get these nutcase assignments because I'm good at them. Maybe I'm some kind of über-interdimensional ninja, the best at flitting betwixt and between, from a real place to one that's a shade more notional. Notional, at least, to us. To a fairy or a yeti it is their world which is real and ours which is imaginary.

After giving herself a rewarding pat on the back for her interdimensional flexibility, Sandrine realized not just one but three things of great import.

One: The green door called Pomme Verte lay just beyond her left foot and was shut. Sandrine did not remember shutting it. As much as she wanted to continue experiencing Vienna's life, the thought of opening the door again made her feel nauseous. Maybe another day.

Two: Sandrine hadn't been made privy to the scene in which Vienna and River built the cabin and then fucked in it. Or maybe they'd fucked in it while they'd been building it. Or perhaps they'd screwed in the dewy grass and then built the walls around that very spot. Whichever it was, she hadn't seen it, and whether she'd admitted it to herself or not, that had been a big part of why she'd opened the green door in the first place. To watch.

Talk about self-punishment, Sardine. Just as well you didn't get what you wanted.

If she wanted to see more, she'd have to open the door again. She felt quite sure that the adjacent door, an appealing shade of purple, would lead to an entirely new story, perhaps one in which happy fish swam amongst the stars, lazily teaching them the alphabet. Of course, a story being lodged behind a bedroom door didn't mean it was true, just magic and mysterious. Magic and mystery implied a kind of truth to be sure, but not the same as objectively factual truth.

If such a thing even existed.

Sandrine, because of her mountaineering, had a more flexible view of reality than most, but it was currently being stretched.

A lot.

A lovely image, Sardine. Fish teaching stars the alphabet. You should go home and tell it to the Sandys. Add some pictures. Write it down. They'll thank you later, if not today.

"I would," she said aloud, "but I can't get up. I'm way too whacked."

Sandrine felt like she'd been away for a million years.

Even more so than when she'd first come down from the mountain.

Three: By far the worst issue was what she actually had seen. It wasn't her husband and best friend having sex, as she'd thought it would be. "Serves me right for wanting to see that," she said.

Sandrine had seen her son. The same one she'd seen this morning. The one she'd run away to Vienna's to forget about.

He was tall and had red hair. His name was Theo.

In some world, somewhere, her son Theo had given Vienna tea and whiskey and fire when she'd been at her worst, things Sandrine herself hadn't done, too angry about her friend's sexual betrayal.

Theo lived nearby, near Hartwood, or he had, before he'd gone away to school in Montreal. He'd had a little friend who wore striped socks, cheap canvas sneakers and an incredible skirt hand sewn out of mullein leaves.

He missed his mom.

In dreams Sandrine was a participant, sometimes even a conscious one, and this hadn't been like that. It was a process of watching, more like a movie. At the same time, Vienna hadn't been exactly like the Vienna she knew. As well, Sandrine still didn't have much in the way of memories of Theo, as though the problem wasn't that she'd forgotten him, but that he lived in a parallel dimension. She hadn't forgotten him because she'd fallen and hurt her head, but because the reality in which he was her son was only beginning to breach her home reality now.

Was it a good idea or a bad idea to want to know one's children who only existed in other worlds?

She'd liked him so much.

Something poked into Sandrine's back.

"Ow!" she shrieked.

"Well," Vienna asked, withdrawing her burgundy shod toe, "did you see anything interesting behind Pomme Verte?"

And then she bent to help Sandrine up.

That was pretty much Vienna, all over. How could Sandrine have forgotten?

Really, she ought to be grateful. It meant Vienna was further along on her road to recovery. Vienna being a bitch was better than Vienna sleeping in a Styrofoam igloo in the swamp.

"I ought to bring over more people for you to abuse," Sandrine said, clambering to her feet with Vienna's help. "It seems to do you a world of good."

Vienna grinned.

"Stop being mean," Sandrine said. "Sooner or later River will wonder why I didn't come home and come looking for me. And then you'll be in real trouble."

Vienna laughed. "You think?" she asked.

It was true. Maybe if River came over it would be to have sex with Vienna and not to save Sandrine from her mad friend at all.

Sandrine let go of her friend's hand and made for the back stairs.

"Turn around," Vienna ordered.

"No," Sandrine said.

"Oh," Vienna said, "but I think you will." Her chunky heels ground the dirt on the unswept kitchen stairs. Sandrine could hear it, as well as her hard voice. Why couldn't she disobey Vienna? Reluctantly, she turned around.

Vienna handed her a green hardbound book.

"Both true love and the lost manuscript," Sandrine said wonderingly, stepping backward with the book in hand.

She fell all the way down the stairs without letting go. It was the same book Theo had given Vienna at the campfire in the swamp. She recognized it not just because of the embossed design but by the looped brown rings of coffee stains on the cover.

At the top of the stairs, Vienna laughed.

If there were cell phones in this world and not just pop tarts, I'd call River and get him to come and pick me up. As things stand, all I can do is lie here and wait for Vienna to come to her senses and take me to the emergency room or call an ambulance. Maybe I'll read while I'm at it.

Her hands were alright, it was her left leg that wasn't. Sandrine opened the impossibility of a green book handed to her from a dream and began to read.

A PARTIAL LIST OF SNUGGLY BOOKS

LÉON BLOY *The Tarantulas' Parlor and Other Unkind Tales*

S. HENRY BERTHOUD *Misanthropic Tales*

FÉLICIEN CHAMPSAUR *The Latin Orgy*

FÉLICIEN CHAMPSAUR *The Emerald Princess
and Other Decadent Fantasies*

BRENDAN CONNELL *Metrophilias*

QUENTIN S. CRISP *Blue on Blue*

QUENTIN S. CRISP *September*

LADY DILKE *The Outcast Spirit and Other Stories*

BERIT ELLINGSEN *Vessel and Solsvart*

EDMOND AND JULES DE GONCOURT *Manette Salomon*

RHYS HUGHES *Cloud Farming in Wales*

JUSTIN ISIS *Divorce Procedures for the Hairdressers of a Metallic
and Inconstant Goddess*

VICTOR JOLY *The Unknown Collaborator and Other Legendary Tales*

BERNARD LAZARE *The Mirror of Legends*

JEAN LORRAIN *Masks in the Tapestry*

JEAN LORRAIN *Nightmares of an Ether-Drinker*

JEAN LORRAIN *The Soul-Drinker and Other Decadent Fantasies*

CAMILLE MAUCLAIR *The Frail Soul and Other Stories*

CATULLE MENDÈS *Bluebirds*

LUIS DE MIRANDA *Who Killed the Poet?*

OCTAVE MIRBEAU *The Death of Balzac*

DAMIAN MURPHY *Daughters of Apostasy*

KRISTINE ONG MUSLIM *Butterfly Dream*

YARROW PAISLEY *Mendicant City*

DAVID RIX *A Suite in Four Windows*

FREDERICK ROLFE *An Ossuary of the North Lagoon and Other Stories*

JASON ROLFE *An Archive of Human Nonsense*

BRIAN STABLEFORD *Spirits of the Vasty Deep*

DOUGLAS THOMPSON *The Fallen West*

TOADHOUSE *Living and Dying in a Mind Field*

www.ingramcontent.com/pod-product-compliance
Lightning Source LLC
Chambersburg PA
CBHW032041180726
48284CB00008B/2696